P9-DFK-218

 THE TEXAS TATTLER

All the news that's barely fit to print!

Honeymoon Horror

Danger was the last thing honeymooners Dawson and Matilda Fortune Prescott expected on a rustic getaway following their lovely whirlwind marriage. But wedding bells turned to gunshots when the new Mrs. Prescott went for a woodsy walk.

"I heard a twig snap behind me, then a bullet zinged past my head and landed in a tree," Matilda told *The Tattler.* "I was terrified and I guess I fainted."

Inside the log cabin love nest her new hubby heard shots and raced outside to find his wife slumped on the forest floor. She was uninjured. Police extracted a pistol bullet from a tree, but they have no other hard evidence. Notorious Red Rock ruffian Clint Lockhart tops the list of suspects. Lockhart holds a longtime grudge against the Fortunes that festered into heinous acts once before when he was convicted of murdering Sophia Fortune. Lockhart escaped prison a few months ago and remains at large.

"I know Lockhart is to blame. And he will pay mightily," Dawson told reporters.

In related news, it seems that Willa Simms, godchild to mogul Ryan Fortune, has gone missing...and so has "bodyguard" Griffin Fortune, brother to Matilda. Sources confirm that their disappearance is related to the shooting. Does their hiding out foretell another close call—for a Fortune's bachelorhood?

 Meet the Fortunes of Texas

Griffin Fortune: He was just doing his job—keeping lovely professor Willa Simms safely hidden away in a cozy mountain cabin. But the longer he was secluded with her, the harder it became to guard his untouchable heart against her beguiling innocence.

Willa Simms: She had never felt anything as overwhelming as her passion for the covert operative. But she was a woman who wanted home and hearth and he dodged danger on a daily basis. Would love overcome their differences so they could make a life *together*?

Teddy Fortune: The family patriarch longed for his sons and daughter to find the same happiness he has in his own marriage to their mother. Dare he hope that his fondest wish would come true?

TO LOVE AND
Protect Her

MARGARET WATSON

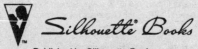

Published by Silhouette Books
America's Publisher of Contemporary Romance

Special thanks and acknowledgment are given to
Margaret Watson for her contribution to
THE FORTUNES OF TEXAS series.

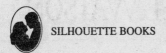 SILHOUETTE BOOKS

TO LOVE AND PROTECT HER

ISBN 0-373-21749-8

Copyright © 1999 by Harlequin Books S.A.

Visit Silhouette Books at www.eHarlequin.com

Printed in U.S.A.

About the Author

MARGARET WATSON

is a passionate reader who has always loved romance. Even when she was reading Nancy Drew books, she was fascinated by Nancy's relationship with Ned. When she outgrew Nancy Drew, she moved on to Mary Stewart, Victoria Holt and Helen MacInnes. Then she discovered Georgette Heyer, and she's never looked back. Margaret is a voracious reader who loves just about any kind of book, but romance and romantic suspense have always been her favorites. She loves exploring the intricacies of relationships and is a sucker for a happy ending. She began writing more than eleven years ago and realized immediately that it was what she wanted to do for the rest of her life.

Margaret lives in Naperville, Illinois, with her husband and three daughters. She is fortunate enough to be involved in two careers that she loves. When she's not writing or spending time with her family, she practices veterinary medicine in Chicago. But writing is definitely her first love. She spends as much time as she can at her computer, working on her stories. When people ask why she does both, she tells them that veterinary medicine is her job, but writing is her passion. And being a romantic through and through, she always follows her heart.

For Bill, who makes all of my dreams come true.

One

This was the last place Griffin Fortune wanted to be.

He sat in his truck outside Willa Simms's apartment, staring at the door of the upscale, quietly tasteful building, and reflected that those qualities could also perfectly describe Willa. Which was why he didn't want to be here. Willa Simms was way out of his league.

But he had promised his uncle, Ryan Fortune, that he would take a look at Willa's security system and make sure she was all right, so he'd driven the two hours into College Station from the Fortune's Double Crown Ranch. It was the least he could do for Ryan, who had been a generous host to the recently discovered Australian branch of the Fortune family.

He'd only be here for a few hours, he told himself. For a few hours, he could ignore the way Willa stirred his blood. Self-control was second nature to him. And if he found that self-control strained whenever he was around Willa, no one else needed to know.

The glow from the streetlights glistened on the rain-slicked pavement as he watched the door to her apartment. "The place looks safe enough to me," he muttered to himself. He scowled at the attractive, sturdy building. But he wouldn't leave without checking it out thoroughly. He'd given Ryan his word, and Griff always kept his promises.

"Might as well get it over with. Hell!" he exclaimed as he stepped out of the truck and into the cold drizzle. "December is a damn uncomfortable season in Texas."

He had just stepped away from his truck when the door of the apartment building burst open from the inside. Two housepainters dressed in white overalls and with painter's caps pulled down low over their faces, hurried out the door. They carried a rolled-up rug between them, and they seemed to be in a hurry.

Who wouldn't be, on a night like this? Griff thought sourly. Out of habit, he watched as the painters headed in the opposite direction. Even when he was off duty, he paid attention to his surroundings.

As the painters approached the side of the building, the rug they carried began to wriggle. Griff narrowed his eyes and, without thinking, began to run.

"Hey, there," he shouted at the painters. "What are you doing?"

The person in the front glanced back at him, then raised his hand and smashed something down on the rug. It stopped wriggling, and Griff broke into a sprint.

He was gaining on the painters and their burden. They struggled to move faster, but it was clear to Griff that whatever they carried was heavy, and it was slowing them down. As he got closer, the person in the lead took one more look at him and said something to the other person. Then they dropped the rug and ran.

They jumped into a dark blue van that had no windows and no signs on the doors. Griff squinted to read the license number, but the van was too far away and the light was too dim. He was reluctant to leave the rug and its contents lying on the cold, damp ground.

The van tore out of the parking lot, its tires squealing, and disappeared into the night. He watched it leave with a flash of regret that he hadn't been able to stop the two housepainters. Then he bent down to examine the rolled-up rug that was now lying in a puddle of water.

Although it was no longer moving, it was roughly the size and shape of a person, and Griff's heart began to pound. What had he interrupted? As he unrolled the carpet, a throaty moan from inside the bundle made him freeze for a moment. Then his hands flew as he pulled the carpet apart.

"Willa!" He stared in shock at Ryan Fortune's goddaughter. She lay still and unmoving, her face pale and her eyes closed. Her glasses dangled from her right ear, the frame bent and twisted. There was a nasty gash over her left ear, and a trickle of blood trailed down her cheek. A lump was already forming around the cut.

"Willa, can you hear me?" he asked, placing his hand on her neck. Her pulse felt strong and steady, and his own heart rate steadied a bit.

She moaned again, and her eyelashes began to flutter. "No!" she cried. He heard the terror in her voice, and damned the two people who had done this to her.

"It's all right, Willa. Those two men are gone. I'm Griffin Fortune. Do you remember me?"

Her eyes slowly opened, and she stared at him, her blue-gray gaze unfocused. "Griff?" she whispered.

"Right. It's Griff." He subdued the ridiculous surge of pleasure that she had remembered him. "Can you sit up?"

She stared at him for a moment, then nodded. She winced immediately, and a murderous rage swept over him. "Let me help you."

He wrapped his arm around her shoulder, forbidding himself to think about how soft she felt, and how well she fit into his embrace. Willa had been injured, for God's sake. "Easy does it, mate."

She closed her eyes and clung to him, and he realized that her coat was soaking wet. The water from the puddle had seeped through the rug. He'd have to get her inside as quickly as possible. He didn't want her to get chilled in the cold rain.

"Can you stand up?" he asked, glancing toward the parking lot. He half expected the blue van to reappear at any moment, and he wanted to be safely away from the apartment before that happened.

"I think so."

She held on to him and pulled herself to her feet. Griff saw her grimace, reflecting a spasm of pain, and his admiration for Willa increased. She was apparently a lot tougher than she seemed to be.

"That's the way, Blue."

She gave him a quizzical look, then took a step toward her apartment. She stopped immediately, and Griff saw her swaying on her feet. "I seem to be a bit unsteady," she said, her voice faint. "Could you help me into my apartment, Mr. Fortune?"

"I don't think that's such a good idea," he said, watching for the blue van. "And what's with the Mr. Fortune stuff? It was Griff just a few moments ago."

A faint red color washed her cheeks. "You can hardly hold me responsible for what I said after I had fainted."

"We'll discuss that later," he said, slipping his arm around her again. Once again, a sense of rightness swept over him. He told himself to ignore it. "And just for the record, you didn't faint. Someone coshed you over the head."

The red disappeared from her face, leaving her pale and puzzled looking. "Why would someone do that? And why am I out here, and all wet?"

"Let's get in out of the rain," he said, urging her toward his truck. He didn't want to go back into her apartment. He had no idea what or who he might find waiting for them.

When she saw that he was leading her away from the apartment rather than toward it, she stopped. "Where are we going?"

"Let's go sit in my truck for a few minutes. It's warm there."

"All right." Without question, she turned and let him lead her toward the truck. Her complete trust shook him. Willa had better learn not to be so trusting, he thought harshly. Her enemies—and apparently she had some—would use that against her.

He helped her into the truck, then got in on the driver's side and locked the door. Turning the heat on full blast, he began to unbutton her coat.

"What are you doing?" she asked, pushing his hands away.

"Your coat is wet. You need to take it off and put on something dry."

He eased the wet wool off her shoulders, then shrugged out of his own worn leather jacket. He wrapped it around her shoulders, and she seemed to burrow into it. "Is that better?" he asked gruffly.

"Mmm."

Gently he pushed the hair away from the cut on her head, and felt his mouth tightening again. The gash had stopped bleeding already, but the skin around it was swollen and bruised. "Do you remember what happened, Willa?"

She looked over at him, and he saw the confusion in her gorgeous blue-gray eyes. "I'm not sure."

"You have your coat on. Were you going into your apartment, or leaving?"

She stared at him, and he saw her effort as she tried to remember. "I was coming home from the university," she finally said. "I got my mail from my mailbox, and I was walking up the stairs."

"Then what happened?"

"I don't know," she said slowly. "There were painters in the hall. They were painting the wall, and they said something to me. That's all I remember."

"Do you remember what they said?"

"No." She tried to shake her head, and winced with pain.

He reached out and took her hand, telling himself she needed someone to hold on to. He didn't want to examine his need to touch her, to reassure himself. "Did you go into your apartment?" Was there someone in there still, waiting for her?

"I don't know. All I remember is seeing the painters and hearing their voices. I don't remember anything else until I heard your voice."

She flushed pink again, and he wondered why. Then she turned to him. "What are you doing here, Mr. Fortune?"

"I like it better when you call me Griff," he said, and he gave her a quick smile. "We're not very formal down in Australia. And I'm here because your godfather asked me to check on your security system. He was worried about you."

Willa eased herself carefully back against the seat and turned to face him. "I mentioned that I'd been getting hang-up phone calls, and he got upset. He wanted me to get a security system, and I told him I would. I didn't think he'd get you involved."

"It's a good thing he did. If I hadn't been here, you'd have been kidnapped."

He regretted his blunt words when she paled again. "Why would anyone want to kidnap me? It's not as if I have anything anyone wants. I'm not a famous person, and I don't have any money."

"Maybe it was just a random attack," he said, although he doubted it. It sounded as if the supposed painters had been waiting for Willa. He didn't want to remind her that her godfather had a lot of money. "The reason doesn't matter, though. It happened, and now we have to decide what to do about it."

"We should go back into my apartment and call the police," Willa said.

"No. We're not going back into your apartment."

"Why not?"

"Because we don't know who those two were, or if they had any help. There may be someone waiting for you in your apartment."

She stared at him, fear welling in her eyes. "I hadn't thought of that."

"I did." His voice was grim. "We need to get away from here. I don't want to be around if those two come back to finish the job they started. Let's get you to a hospital."

He put the truck in gear and pulled out of the parking lot. He didn't like the smell of this. His sister Matilda had been shot at and almost killed while she was on her honeymoon. Everyone had suspected Clint Lockhart was involved, but so far they couldn't prove anything. He didn't know if the attack on Willa was connected, but he wasn't going to take any chances.

Even though Clint was Ryan's brother-in-law by his first wife and therefore one of the family, he'd held a grudge against the Fortunes for years. He believed they had stolen his father's ranch out from under him, taking advantage of his financial difficulties. His desire for revenge had caused him to plot with

Ryan's estranged wife Sophia in an effort to exhort money from Ryan. When things went sour, he'd killed Sophia. He'd escaped from prison several months ago, and the family had lived in fear ever since.

Yes, until he had some answers, he was going to stick close to Willa.

"Where's the nearest hospital?" he asked her as he waited to turn onto the street.

"I don't need to go to a hospital." Her voice sounded stronger, and she touched the lump on her head. He saw her wince, even in the dim light. "It's just a lump on the head."

"You should probably get it checked."

"I'm fine, Griff." She touched it again. "They'll just tell me to take two aspirins and call them in the morning." She gave him a weak smile, and his heart rate increased. Even injured and frightened, she was able to make a joke at her own expense.

He didn't want to go to the hospital, either, but for a different reason. He was afraid that the kidnappers would be expecting them to go to a hospital, and be waiting there for them. And he didn't want to take that chance. With the medical training he'd had as part of his job he could probably tend to Willa's injuries. "Are you sure?" he asked.

"Positive." Her voice was firm. "Let's go call the police."

He hesitated. "I'm not sure we should do that."

"Why not?" She turned in her seat toward him, and he saw the bewilderment in her face. "Someone tried to kidnap me. Why wouldn't we call the police?''

"I'm not used to relying on the police," he finally said. "But maybe you're right. We should let them know. The kidnappers might come back to your apartment. The police can at least keep an eye out for them."

He pulled over to the side of the road and took his cellular phone out of his jacket pocket. He had to bend close to Willa to reach it, and her scent curled around him. It wasn't the demure floral scent he would have expected. It was sharp and tangy, reminding him of wild, elemental things that he had no business connecting with Willa.

He leaned as far away from her as he could and dialed 9-1-1. When the police answered, he told them what had happened, gave them a description of the van and the two kidnappers, then told them he was taking Willa away to keep her safe. He didn't tell them where he was going. Cutting off their sputtering questions, he snapped the phone closed and set it on the floor.

"Okay, we've called the police."

Willa had leaned back against the seat and closed her eyes while he talked. Now she opened them and gave him a tiny grin. "That's not exactly what I had in mind. You didn't give them a lot to work with."

"I told them as much as we knew."

"Didn't they want to talk to me?"

"They did." He scowled at her. "But I'm not letting anyone close to you until we figure out who tried to snatch you, and why. Not even the police.''

Willa felt a soft warmth stealing over her as she looked at Griff. His hard face was even harder than usual, and his mouth was set in a grim line. He looked formidable and dangerous, and the wild part of him, the part that had drawn her from the first time she met him, was very close to the surface.

''Then what are we going to do?'' She was amazed at how calm she sounded. But she trusted him completely, she realized. Griff would keep her safe.

''We're going to leave,'' he said slowly. ''We're going to go somewhere that no one will expect us to go. Somewhere far from College Station and your godfather's ranch.''

''You don't think Ryan has anything to do with this, do you?'' She was horrified.

''Of course not. But that's where someone would expect you to go, isn't it?''

''Probably,'' she said reluctantly. ''He's the only family I have.''

''Then we're going in the opposite direction.'' He glanced at his watch, then pulled the truck away from the curb. ''Ryan told me about a little cabin in the mountains near El Paso that his sister-in-law Mary Ellen owns. Her son used it recently, and it sounded quiet and isolated—perfect for hiding. We're going to try and find it.''

''El Paso is a long way from here,'' she said faintly.

He glanced over at her in the darkness of the truck.

"Would you rather not go that far with me? I'd understand. You don't really know me that well."

She knew him well enough to trust him completely, she realized. She had no hesitation about going to El Paso, or anywhere else, with Griff. "It's not that. I've just never taken off like this before, without planning ahead of time. I've never been a really spontaneous kind of person."

"I'm sure I can think of somewhere else to go."

"No. El Paso is fine." A recklessness she didn't recognize swept over her. "The farther the better."

His mouth curled into a tiny grin. "For someone who's never been a really spontaneous kind of person, I'd say you're doing just fine."

"You'll keep me safe, Griff. I'm not worried about that."

"What about your job? Don't you have to teach at the university?"

"Classes are off for Christmas break. So no one will miss me. I can go wherever I want to go."

"Being a loner isn't always a good thing."

She glanced over at him and his mouth was a tight line.

"If those two had succeeded," he continued, "how long would it have been before you were missed?"

That was something she didn't want to think about. "Are you saying I should be checking in with someone on a regular basis?"

"It wouldn't hurt."

"Who do you check in with, Griff?" Her voice

held just the right amount of polite enquiry, she thought with satisfaction.

His mouth tightened further. "That's different. I know how to take care of myself."

"So do I. You probably don't know it, but I traveled the world with my father while I was growing up." She felt the same pull of grief and pain that always came when she talked about her father. "I learned very early how to take care of myself."

"That's not what I meant, and you know it." His voice was rough. "I'm talking about protecting yourself."

"I've taken a self-defense class. I know what to do."

"It sure helped tonight, didn't it."

She looked away from him and stared out the window. Already the town was falling behind them, and the car passed rolling hills and open pasture. Her home and her job were behind them. And she hoped the kidnappers were, as well. "Now that I know someone wants to kidnap me, I'll be prepared. I'll be more alert."

She heard him sigh. "Sorry, Willa. I didn't mean to pick on you. And you're not going to have to worry about being alone for a while. As long as those kidnappers are around, I'm going to be with you until we find out who they are, and catch them."

A flash of pleasure warmed her, surprising her with its intensity. Willa tried to tell herself that it wasn't a big deal, that Griff was just doing her godfather, Ryan, a favor, but it didn't matter. The thought of spending the next few days alone with Griff Fortune made her blood heat in her veins.

But she wasn't Griff's type of woman, she reminded herself. Griff, she was sure, was interested in worldly, sophisticated women—the kind of women who traveled in the same circles as he did. Rumors in the Fortune family said Griff was some kind of secret agent. A man like that wouldn't want to get involved with a quiet, homebody university professor like her.

And a quiet university professor shouldn't be interested in a man like Griff.

The rebellious part of her, the part that wasn't sure she liked being a university professor, yearned for the wildness of Griff's life. The part of her that had loved traveling around the world, loved the adventure of life with her father, said Griff was exactly the kind of man she was interested in. But she ignored it. If she listened to that voice, it would be a betrayal of her father and everything he wanted for her.

"We have a long ride ahead of us." Griff's voice came out of the darkness again. "And you had a rough night. Why don't you try to get some rest?"

"It's hard to sleep in a car," she said. "I always wake up with a stiff neck."

"You can rest your head on my shoulder. That way I can check you frequently to make sure you don't have a concussion." He cleared his throat. "Go ahead and relax."

"That would be uncomfortable for you."

"I'll survive." There was a grimness to his voice

she didn't understand. "One of us might as well get some sleep."

"I *am* a little tired," she said, and she heard the weariness in her own voice.

"Then come on, Blue. Close your eyes."

She curled up on the seat, adjusted her seat belt, and leaned against his shoulder. His muscles were tense and hard beneath her ear, and when she shifted around, she felt him tremble. But the rumble of the truck's engine soothed her, and the warmth of Griff's body surrounded her—she felt herself relaxing.

"Why did you call me Blue?" she asked, her voice sleepy.

"It's an Australian nickname for someone with red hair."

His voice washed over her, and she snuggled closer. She felt him tense again, and then his hand stroked over her hair. "Go to sleep, Willa."

"Keep talking to me," she said, tucking her hand under his arm. "Why do Australians call people with red hair 'Blue'? That sounds kind of contrary."

"That's because Australians are contrary." She heard the smile in his voice. "Blue is also what we call an argument. I guess people think that redheads are more likely to get into arguments."

"I think that's unfair. I'm very even tempered."

"Is that right?" He stroked her hair again, and she wanted to arch into his touch. "I'll remember you said that next time you're giving me grief over my protecting you."

She imagined that he touched her hair again, very

lightly, and she thought his hand lingered on her head. She wanted to beg him not to stop, but she clamped her mouth firmly shut. It was the blow to the head, she told herself. It was making her want things she knew she couldn't have. It made her yearn for what couldn't be.

Silence filled the car again. "Don't stop talking," she said, and her voice was drowsy with sleep. "I love to listen to you. Your accent is so musical."

"I don't have an accent, mate," he said, exaggerating his drawl. "It's you Yanks who talk funny."

She smiled and allowed herself to drift to the place between sleep and wakefulness. "Tell me about your sister. I like her so much."

"She's something, our Matilda is." Willa heard the love mixed with resignation in his voice. "She's a handful. It took me and all four of my brothers to keep an eye on her."

"I bet she loved that."

"She's a lot like you, Willa. She was sure she could take care of herself, too."

"I know her well enough to know that she can." She was too tired to rise to his bait. "Can you tell me about Australia?"

He hesitated, then he began speaking in a low, soothing voice, describing the beauty of his country. As she drifted off to sleep, she realized that he was deliberately lulling her, but she didn't care. Her head still hurt, and she was exhausted. And although she was driving through the night to an unknown destination with a man she didn't know all that well, she felt amazingly content.

She was with Griff, and that was all that mattered.

Two

"Wake up, Willa."

The voice intruded on her dreams, and she closed her eyes more firmly and tried to hang on as the dream faded into the mist. She was dreaming about Griff, and his hand was drawing a long, lazy line down her back. She didn't want to wake up, didn't want the dream to end.

"Come on, Willa, it's time to wake up."

It was Griff's voice, and his hand was touching her shoulder. Slowly she opened her eyes. She was lying on his lap, and his brown eyes were looking down at her, concern in their warm depths.

She scrambled to sit up. "Griff?" She pushed her hair out of her eyes and stared at him. "What are you doing here? And where are we?"

"We're in El Paso—" he began.

"El Paso!" she gasped. "What are we doing in El Paso?"

He hesitated. "Don't you remember what happened last night?"

Last night. Suddenly all the events of the night before came flooding back. "I had forgotten," she whispered.

"How's your head?"

She touched the lump on her left temple. "It hurts," she said. "But I'm sure I'll survive."

He worked his jaw. "I'll take care of it when we get to the cabin. I thought we'd stop in here first and get some groceries and other things we'll need."

She looked out the window of the truck and saw that they were in the parking lot of a store that advertised one-stop shopping. "All right."

Before she could get out of the car, Griff laid his hand on her arm. Her skin heated and her heart raced, but Griff didn't seem to notice a thing.

"I'm not going to say anything in the store," he said. "We don't want anyone remembering the bloke with the funny accent."

Willa felt herself pale as she looked at him. "Do you think the kidnappers could have followed us from College Station?"

"No one followed us. I'm sure of that. But we don't want to take any chances, so I'm keeping my mouth shut."

He drew his hand away, and Willa felt bereft. She wanted to reach for him, but instead curled her fingers into her palm. She'd better get hold of herself. She was going to be spending a lot of time with Griff.

They went through the store quickly, loading their shopping cart with food and a couple of changes of clothes for each of them. Willa grabbed toiletries, as well as a handful of books to read.

In a half hour they were back in the truck. Griff's hands tightened on the steering wheel, and he didn't look at Willa. "I have to call Ryan and get directions to the cabin," he said. "Are you sure you want to do this?"

"Are you having second thoughts?" she asked. "I didn't even think to ask if you could spare the time to stay with me."

"My time isn't a problem," he said, his voice short. "I want to be sure you understand that we're going to be alone together, possibly for a while. Are you sure you don't want to go somewhere else?"

She was too aware of Griff, sitting so close to her in the car. Surrounded by his male scent, his leather jacket still wrapped around her shoulders, her senses were overwhelmed with him. The air around them pulsated with tension. Spending time alone with Griff would be dangerous.

"I'm sure," she said.

Griff studied Willa for a moment. Her eyes were heavy with fatigue and the bruise on her temple stood out sharply on her pale face. But he saw the resolution in her eyes and nodded with approval. "Good. I'll call Ryan, then."

Willa was a lot tougher than he'd suspected, he reflected as he listened to the phone connecting. She was a lady, and he hadn't spent much time around ladies in his life. He had been prepared for tears and a quivering fearfulness. But Willa had just lifted her chin and given him a steady look. He was almost ready to believe her when she said she could take care of herself.

Almost, but not quite.

She was too trusting, too good-hearted to be as wary as she needed to be. She probably trusted anyone who didn't actually wave a gun in her face, he thought cynically. If anyone needed a keeper, it was Willa Simms.

He wanted nothing more than to volunteer for the job.

And wouldn't that be a sight. Wild Griffin Fortune, with his dubious personal background and his present unsavory job, involved with genteel Willa Simms, university professor.

If it weren't so ludicrous, his fantasy would be good for a laugh. As it was, it was merely pathetic.

He had absolutely nothing in common with Willa. As if to remind him of that fact, his Uncle Ryan's voice came on the phone.

"Ryan, it's Griff. We've run into a bit of trouble."

"What is it?" Griff could imagine Ryan sitting up straight in his chair, his eyebrows drawn together.

Griff quickly explained what had happened at Willa's the night before. "We're in another part of the state now," he said, aware that it was all too easy to eavesdrop on a cellular phone call. "I remember you mentioned a cabin that Mary Ellen owns. The one that Jace used recently. Could you give me directions?"

"Of course." Ryan told him how to get to the isolated cabin, being careful not to mention any names that could give away their location. And he told him obliquely where the key was hidden. Ryan was quick, Griff thought with appreciation.

"We're going to stay there for a while. You might want to get some investigators into College Station, see what they can find out. I'd rather not expose Willa to another kidnapping attempt."

"Thank God you got to her apartment when you did."

Griff could hear the emotion in Ryan's voice.

"Are you sure she's all right?"

"She will be. Your goddaughter is tough," he said.

There must have been surprise in his voice, because Ryan laughed. "Damn right, she's tough. She gets that from her old man. He was one hard guy. Let me talk to her."

He handed the phone to Willa and watched her as she listened to Ryan. Her eyes softened and her mouth trembled as she smiled. Finally she said, "I'm fine, Ryan, and so is Griff. I hope you don't mind if we use Mary Ellen's cabin."

She smiled again as she listened, and a low laugh gurgled out of her throat. Its husky sound wound its way inside him and seemed to take hold. He wanted to hear that laugh of Willa's again.

Smiling, she said goodbye and handed him the phone. "Ryan says he trusts you with my life."

Griff scowled, irritated by his inability to control his desire for Willa. "He knows damn well he can trust me with your life. I'd never let a family member down."

Willa's smile faded a little. "I'm glad you take your family obligations so seriously." She shifted to stare out the window of the truck, but he'd caught the hurt in her eyes before she turned away.

Griff watched her stiff back, felt the tension swirling through the cab of the truck, and sighed. "Hell, Willa, you know I didn't mean it that way."

"Do I? I know practically nothing about you," she retorted. "And for the record, you don't owe me any explanations." Her voice was cool, and she didn't turn around. "We're in an unfortunate situation, but that doesn't mean that I'll intrude in your life. You can be sure I won't be a burden."

She was as far from a burden as he could imagine, and he wanted nothing more than to have Willa intrude in his life. The realization brought a knot to his gut. He gripped the steering wheel more tightly. "Willa, I wouldn't have brought you here to El Paso if I didn't care what happened to you. If I were just doing a favor for Ryan, I would have taken you back to the Double Crown Ranch. I didn't mean it that way."

Willa turned around and looked at him, but her eyes were carefully blank. "I'm sorry if I misunderstood, Griff. Shouldn't we be on our way?"

He swore silently as he put the truck into gear and pulled out of the parking lot a little more quickly than he should have. "You're right. We don't want to stay here long enough to give anyone a chance to remember us."

They rode in silence for a while, tension still thick between them. He was shocked to realize that he wanted to pull Willa into his arms and show her just how much he cared about what happened to her. Telling himself again that he was too rough and untamed for a woman like Willa, he drummed his fingers on the steering wheel and listened to the hum of the tires on the asphalt.

Taking Willa to this cabin, staying alone there with her, was a huge mistake. He should have known better. He'd known from the first time he saw Willa that she would be trouble. He hadn't been able to take his eyes off her. And now he was going to be cooped up with her in a tiny cabin, with nothing else to do but look at her. And talk to her.

He should turn around right now and go back to the Double Crown Ranch.

But he couldn't take any chances with her, so he continued on the route out of El Paso. When the road began climbing into the mountains, he forced himself to say to her, "Have you ever been to this part of Texas?"

"No," she answered. Her voice was carefully even, and he couldn't interpret her tone. "Before I moved to College Station, the only part of Texas I'd visited was the Double Crown and San Antonio."

"Keep an eye on the area," he said gruffly. "You never know when you'll need to find your way around here."

Her eyes widened as she stared at him. "What do you mean?"

She seemed more puzzled than shocked, and he sighed at her naiveté. "We don't know what's going to happen in the next several days. I want you to be prepared for anything.''

He felt her eyes on him, studying him. ''I think I understand what Ryan meant,'' she finally said slowly. ''Don't worry, Griff. I could get us back to El Paso if I had to, if that's what you're worried about.''

''What did Ryan say?'' he asked, unable to stop himself.

To his surprise, a faint smile played around her lips. ''He said that you always think three steps ahead of everyone else. He said that you'd managed to surprise even him. Now I understand what he meant. I can practically see you thinking as you drive, preparing for any possibility.''

''I learned a long time ago that you only survive if you're smarter than your enemy. And I intend for both of us to survive.''

''I already told you that I trust you,'' she said softly. ''I meant it, Griff.''

The coolness was gone from her eyes. Now there was only warmth, and a light that burned steadily as she watched him. It made an answering flame leap inside him.

Deliberately, he turned away to focus on the road. There was no excuse for becoming distracted from his job. And Willa was definitely a distraction.

''According to Ryan, we should be there in about ten minutes,'' he said.

''And then what?''

''Then we wait,'' he said grimly. ''Ryan is putting

some private investigators on the job in College Station to see what they can turn up. We're going to stay here until we have some answers. Until we know who was trying to kidnap you, I don't want to take any chances."

"All right."

He glanced over at her. "All right? As easily as that? What if Ryan doesn't learn anything? You don't have forever before you have to start teaching your classes again. What if we don't know what's going on, and you have to go back to the university?"

"I'm not sure," she said slowly. "Right now, the university and my job there seem very far away. I haven't thought about it once since we left College Station." She turned to him again, and gave him a blinding smile that made his legs weak. "I'm not going to worry about that until I have to."

"I thought you were a regimented, plan-everything kind of woman," he managed to say. "You teach at a university, for God's sake. How much more by-the-book can you get than that? I figured an open-ended stay here in El Paso would be a problem for you."

"I guess you were wrong, then," she said lightly. "Maybe underneath this mousy exterior, I'm really a wild woman."

"Mousy?" He gave her an incredulous look. "You're about as far from mousy as you could get."

His response was instantaneous, and he saw her blush. "Thank you, Griff," she murmured. "But my physical attributes aren't the issue. My job is. And I have a month before I have to worry about it. So let's just forget about it for now.''

''That's fine with me,'' he muttered. How was he supposed to forget her physical attributes? he thought to himself. Especially when she'd spent the night sleeping on his lap.

He hardened again just thinking about it. He'd seen that her head was bent as she slept on his shoulder, and knew she'd awaken with a stiff neck. So he'd eased her down until she rested on his lap. That had been a mistake. It had been a night of pure torture for him, but he wouldn't have traded it for anything. The fragrant cloud of her hair had drifted over his thigh, and whenever he'd shifted, her scent had swirled around him. As she slept, she'd unselfconsciously slid her hand under his leg, and the imprint of her fingers still burned on his skin. Even the heavy denim fabric of his jeans hadn't been a barrier to the sensations. He'd been in a state of arousal for the whole trip, and it still hadn't receded completely.

Which was probably why he was acting like an idiot.

''Here's the road that leads to the cabin,'' he said, as they turned onto a rutted dirt track. He was relieved and grateful for the distraction. ''It doesn't look like anyone has been this way in a while.''

''Great,'' she said fervently. ''I can't wait to get out of this truck.''

Neither could he. The atmosphere was too confined, too intimate. Especially after last night.

But he was afraid that living in the same house with Willa was going to be even more so.

Betsy Keene sat on the shabby couch in the small living area of her trailer near Leather Bucket and shrank back against the cushions. She stared at the man who had been her lover ever since he showed up on her doorstep six months ago, wounded and needing help. Clint Lockhart raged through the room, throwing papers onto the floor and overturning her tiny kitchen table and chairs. His blue eyes were black with rage, and his arrogant mouth, the mouth she'd come to love, was twisted into a frightening grimace.

"We should have had her!" he shouted, slamming his fist onto the counter. The jars and boxes on top of the counter jumped, and so did Betsy. "One more minute, and we would have had her."

"We can try again, Clint," Betsy said, her voice placating.

"When?" He turned on her, his eyes blazing. "When will we get another chance? That meddling son of a bitch Ryan Fortune is going to make sure we can't get close to Willa again. He'll swoop her up and bring her to the Double Crown Ranch, and that will be it. We can't take her from that ranch. Everyone there knows me. And since you started working at the ranch house they know you, too."

"Maybe there's something we can do," she said nervously, pleating the fabric of her dress with shaking fingers. Clint was frightening her. He'd lost his temper before, but this time there was a glaze of madness in his eyes. She prayed he wouldn't turn his rage against her.

"What can we do?" Clint's voice dripped with scorn. "Should I call her on the phone and ask her to meet us somewhere by herself? That snooty, stuck-up college professor is too smart for that." He kicked over a table and sent a lamp crashing into a wall. "She won't be so stuck-up once I get my hands on her."

Fear filled Betsy's mouth with a sour taste as she edged away from Clint. My God, what was wrong with him? Willa Simms had never harmed him, or her, either. In fact, Willa had always been pleasant to her, and very kind.

"Why are you so angry with Willa?" she asked, her voice tentative.

"Because she has what I should have," he shouted at her, his eyes full of rage. "She has free run of the Double Crown. Ryan Fortune gives her anything she wants. That should be *my* ranch. And it would be, too, if Ryan's father hadn't swindled my dad into selling our neighboring ranch to him. I should've inherited the ranch from my father. *I* should be the one in charge. Everyone should kowtow to *me*. I should be the one with all the money. And I will be. I'll get the ranch in the end. We'll see who's smarter, me or Ryan Fortune. He thought he was so smart trying to frame me for Sophia's murder, but I'll show him."

"I know you'll win," Betsy said. She had to soothe him somehow. "You're smarter than Ryan Fortune. Anyone can see that."

"That's right," he said, seeming to calm down at her words. "At least you believe in me, Betsy."

"You know I do, Clint." She licked her lips and watched him carefully. The madness seemed to be fading from his eyes. "You wouldn't really hurt Willa, would you?"

A crafty look came into his eyes. "Now, why would I want to do that? That would be like killing the goose that laid the golden egg, wouldn't it?"

"I knew you were a smart one, Clint. I knew it right away."

Betsy told herself she should be relieved, but fear ate away at her gut. Clint was getting more impatient, more angry every day. And he'd raged at her during the entire trip back from College Station.

"That's right, Betsy. I'm smart enough to figure this out." His mouth twisted again, and once more madness shone out of his eyes. "And who was that man at her apartment who chased us, anyway? Do you know?"

"N-no, Clint, I don't." He'd looked familiar, but she'd been trying to get away and hadn't taken a good look. "He must have been intending to visit someone in the apartment."

Clint's eyes darkened. "I'll teach him to meddle."

"He's probably long gone," Betsy said, watching Clint, the fear roiling inside her. Had Clint gone completely mad? "We won't have to worry about him the next time."

But her words only seemed to infuriate him. "Next

time?'' he screamed. "Next time? How can there be a next time? We should have had her *tonight*."

"Maybe she's at the ranch already." Betsy clutched the fabric of her dress more tightly. She was terribly afraid of what Clint would do to Willa. But she was more afraid of what he would do to her. So she took a breath and said, "If she's at the ranch, I'll get her to come with me. She'd have no reason to be afraid of me. I'll bring her to you."

"What if she's not at the ranch?" Clint asked. Now his eyes looked calculating.

"I'll stick close to Ryan's office," she said, desperate to find some way of appeasing Clint. "She's bound to get in touch with him. I'll listen whenever he gets a phone call. I'll get the information for you. Haven't I always done what you wanted me to do?"

He smiled at her, but there was no warmth in his face, and Betsy shivered. "Yeah, you've always done what I wanted you to do, Betsy. And I won't forget it."

He grabbed his coat from the door and stepped outside. "I need to think for a while. You figure out how you're going to get that information for me."

Clint slammed the door, and the trailer shook for a moment. Betsy slumped against the couch, staring at the door, as tears slowly trickled down her face. *How did everything go so wrong?* she cried to herself. She'd had such glorious dreams of a wonderful life with Clint. Now they were as old and dusty as the dirt of the Double Crown Ranch. And as unattainable.

* * *

She had to put Griff out of her mind, Willa told herself as they bumped along the rutted dirt trail that was supposed to lead to the cabin. The disturbing feelings he roused in her were nothing more than her hormones reacting to an attractive man. Griff wouldn't be interested in a woman like her, a woman who wasn't exciting or glamorous or sophisticated.

She stared out the window, trying to find something else to think about. "The trees along this road to the house are beautiful," she said in a low voice, desperate for an innocuous topic to discuss.

"They're a problem." Griff sounded worried.

She couldn't stop herself from looking over at him. "What do you mean, 'they're a problem'?"

"Too much cover." His face was hard. "Anyone could sneak up on the cabin along this road, and we wouldn't be able to see them until they were at the door."

"Who's going to come to the cabin, Griff?" she asked. "No one but Ryan knows we're here."

He glanced over at her, and she thought his eyes softened a little. "Remember what you said about thinking three steps ahead? That's what I'm trying to do."

"But it's so quiet up here. Surely we would hear anyone driving up the road."

"I hope so." He glanced out the window again. "Damn trees. I don't know why you Americans are so nuts about trees."

"Don't you have trees in Australia?" she asked, trying to keep the laughter from her voice.

"We have plenty of trees," he muttered. "We just don't put them where they don't need to be." When he glanced over at her and saw her smiling, he smiled reluctantly. "We don't have a lot of trees on the Crown Peak Ranch. It's mostly pasture and red dirt. And don't mind me. I'm just worrying out loud."

"I think the trees along the road are beautiful."

He scowled again. "Yeah, they're magnificent."

She turned to look out the window again, her smile fading. Griff took his job very seriously. And she was grateful that he did. She needed to keep that in mind.

"Is your family's Crown Peak Ranch in Australia a lot different than the Double Crown Ranch?" she asked.

"Actually, it's quite similar to the Double Crown," he answered. "Which isn't too surprising, I guess, considering that my father Teddy and Ryan are half brothers."

"Ryan was so excited when he found Teddy." Willa smiled, remembering her godfather's delight. "And he was thrilled that you and Matilda and Reed and Brody could spend this time with him."

"My father was happy about it, too," Griff said. "He'd always wondered about his family."

As they talked, the truck emerged from the last of the trees to a small clearing surrounded by more trees. The mountain rose sharply behind the cabin, but the trees and the rock behind them gave the small clearing a cozy, secluded feel.

The cabin itself was made of weathered logs that blended into the rustic setting. There was a porch that ran the length of the front of the cabin, and a pile of firewood was stacked along one side.

"Let's leave the car here for now, and take a look around," Griff said.

Willa stepped out of the car, and realized that there was a chill to the air. "I had forgotten we'd be in the mountains," she said, pulling Griff's jacket more tightly around herself. Then she looked over at him and realized that he was in his shirtsleeves. He didn't seem to react. He stood measuring the cabin with his eyes, examining the area around it.

Willa reached into the truck and grabbed her wool coat. It was still a little damp from the night before, but she took off Griff's jacket and slipped on her own. She missed the battered jacket immediately. It had smelled and felt like Griff.

"Here, Griff," she said. "It's too cold to stand there without your jacket."

He glanced over at her, and she saw concern flash in his eyes. "Why did you put that coat on? It's still wet."

"It's fine." She thrust his jacket at him, ignoring the feeling of loss. "We're just going into the house, aren't we?"

He took his jacket absently and slipped it on, still studying the area. He was silent for so long that Willa moved closer to him.

"Is something wrong?" she asked.

He looked over at her as if she'd startled him. "Wrong? No, it looks fine."

"You've been staring at the cabin as if you expected it to turn on you."

He gave her a smile and took her hand. "I was just running scenarios in my head. Let's take a look at the back."

It was only a casual gesture, she told herself as he led her around to the back of the cabin. There was no reason for her heart to race in her chest and for her lungs to feel like they were going to explode. Griff was merely trying to shepherd her along, and taking her hand was the quickest way to do it.

But her hand felt so right in his. She wanted to twine their fingers together, to press her palm against his and feel her heart stutter in response.

She'd better get a grip, she told herself harshly. She didn't want to make a fool of herself, or embarrass him. So she forced herself to ignore the feel of his hand on hers, and concentrate on the cabin that would be their home for a while.

There was a small shed at the rear of the cabin, and Griff opened the door. Tools and ladders lined the walls, and there was a space large enough to hold their truck. Otherwise, the shed was empty. Griff shut the door, and they kept walking.

The trees that surrounded the cabin seemed to press in from the back. Griff dropped her hand as he moved into the thicket of woods, and she could almost read his mind. The trees were too close to the house. They could provide too much cover for someone intent on surprising them. Willa shoved her hands into her pockets and shivered. The feelings Griff aroused in her made it too easy to forget the real reason they were at this cabin.

"I don't like this," he said, and she saw the concern in his eyes. "These trees are far too close to the building. But there's nothing we can do about it. I'll rig up an alarm system for these windows at the rear of the cabin. That will help."

"I guess no one thought of this cabin as a hideout from kidnappers," Willa said, trying to keep the snap out of her voice. She was grateful they had a refuge like this cabin.

Griff gave her a quick smile. "The trees can't be helped. But we can fix the problem. Let's go inside."

Willa expected to find a very basic, rustic living space. She was surprised at the comfortable, homey atmosphere inside the cabin. Rugged, oversize furniture was grouped around a magnificent stone fireplace that soared up two stories to an exposed-beam ceiling. There were carpets on the hardwood floors, and pictures and Native American rugs on the walls. The kitchen was small but functional. A table and chairs stood between the kitchen and the living area.

There was one bedroom off the living area. A combination of fear and excitement stirred as she looked inside at the one huge bed it held.

"It's all right," Griff said behind her. "Ryan told me there's another bed in the loft." He nodded to the loft area above the bedroom. "You take the bedroom, and I'll take the loft."

Willa was amazed at the disappointment that snaked through her at Griff's words. As soon as she realized she'd been hoping this would be the only bed in the cabin, she was horrified with herself. Backing out of the room, she said breathlessly, "I'll get the bags from your truck."

"Let me help you."

Griff led the way back out to the truck. It took several trips, but they finally got all the bags of food and supplies into the cabin. Griff drove the truck around the back to put it in the shed, and Willa started to put away the food.

She'd better settle down, she told herself. She and Griff were going to be in this cabin, alone, for God knew how long. If she didn't want to make a complete fool of herself, she'd better remember that Griff was just doing this as a favor to Ryan Fortune. He'd made that clear enough.

Griff came back into the cabin a few minutes later, and carefully locked the door behind him. Then he went over and examined the window in the main room. Willa watched as his fingers traced the frame lightly, brushing over the wood and lingering over the locks. Before she could stop herself, she was imagining Griff's hands on her, exploring her as thoroughly as he explored the window.

Making a disgusted noise under her breath, she turned her back and jerked open another cabinet. But putting the food away couldn't stop her from being aware of Griff in the cabin. She knew instantly when he moved away from the main room and walked into the bedroom.

She refused to allow herself to turn and look at him.

Instead, she called out, "What's the verdict on the security?" She hoped he could hear nothing in her voice aside from friendly concern.

"It'll do." His voice was muffled, as if he were still bent over the window. "I have a few things I want to do, but then it should be all right."

"Did you want something to eat first?"

Griff emerged from the bedroom. "I'll make us a couple of sandwiches in a while. But first I want to take a look at that head of yours."

Willa put her hand on the bump over her left temple. "I'd almost forgotten about this."

"I hadn't." His voice was controlled, and she saw a flash of anger turn his eyes dark. "I want to make sure you're all right."

"I'm fine, Griff." She wasn't sure she wanted Griff to come any closer to her, even if only to check the cut on her head. Her heart was already beating frantically in her ears, and it was hard to draw a breath. "Why don't you take care of the windows, while I make us sandwiches?"

"That will keep. Your injuries won't." He moved toward her.

"I'm fine, Griff. Really." When she realized she was backing away from him, she stopped and straightened. "I'll put some alcohol on the cut and that will take care of it."

"I want to make sure there's nothing else wrong with you. We don't know what they did to you inside your building to get you into that rug."

He wasn't going to take no for an answer. Willa

shrugged. ''All right. You might as well get it over with. But you're not going to find anything wrong.''

Except that her palms were sweating and her heart was thundering in her chest!

Three

"It will only take me a minute," he said. He glanced behind him. "Let's sit down over on the couch."

Willa slipped past Griff in the tiny kitchen and went over to the couch, trying to compose herself. In a few moments, Griff joined her. He was holding a brown bottle and several tubes and packages of bandages.

"You look like you're ready to take care of a whole army," she said.

"I wasn't sure what I would need, so I just got everything I saw in the store."

Willa turned her head so that Griff could see the cut. "Go ahead, then, and get it over with."

Griff didn't move, and finally Willa turned to face him. "What's wrong?"

"Does your head hurt that much?" he asked.

She shook her head. "Of course not."

"Then what's wrong? You're as stiff as a board."

She felt her face heating, but she wasn't about to tell him the truth. She was bracing herself for his touch. She couldn't tell him that her heart was racing and her skin tingling because he was so close to her.

So she shrugged. "I never did like having people poke at me when I was hurt. Go ahead."

She turned her head away, but she felt him hesitate. Finally he touched her face. His hands were as gentle and light as the touch of a butterfly's wings, and when his fingers trailed over the side of her head, lingering at the angle of her jaw, she shivered in response.

"Your cut is beginning to heal already," he said, his voice hoarse. "I'm going to clean it, then leave it alone. I think it'll be fine."

"Good," she managed to say. Swallowing hard, she clamped her hands between her thighs and looked out the window. She knew very well what Griff would see in her face if she looked at him. He would see desire.

She was afraid he would find it pathetic.

So she kept her head turned away as he wiped at the cut with a cold, stinging liquid. "It's alcohol," he said, and he cleared his throat. "I'm sorry if it hurts, but they dropped you in that muddy water. I want to make sure that cut is disinfected."

"Don't worry about it," she managed to say. *Just do this quickly,* she pleaded silently.

After a few moments he moved away from her. Willa started to get up, but Griff laid a hand on her arm.

"Just a minute," he said. "I'm not finished."

"You took care of the cut," she said, telling herself to pull away from him. "What else is there?"

"I don't know." He didn't let go of her arm, and

she didn't try to move away. "But I want to ask you a few questions."

Slowly she sat back down on the couch. "I already told you, I don't remember what happened."

He smiled. Almost as if he couldn't help himself, he reached out and pushed her hair away from the cut on her head. "I know. And I'm not going to push. But I want to make sure they didn't hurt you anyplace else."

Heat trailed down her face, following his fingers, and she swallowed again. "All right."

His hand dropped away from her face, and held hers. "You said you had gotten your mail, and you remember seeing the painters. They said something to you. Did you answer them?"

She closed her eyes and tried to remember, but there was a void. "I don't remember," she said, opening her eyes. "But I probably would have, if they spoke to me."

"You're too polite to ignore someone talking to you." He took her other hand and fixed his gaze on her face. "So they said something to you, you answered them, and they probably moved closer while you talked. Do you remember if they hit you?"

She shook her head slowly. "I don't remember anything after that."

Griff frowned. "If they didn't hit you, they would have to have used something like chloroform to knock you out. Otherwise, they couldn't have gotten you rolled up in that rug. I didn't smell anything when I found you. Does your throat hurt?"

"Not at all."

"Then let's take a look at your head."

He moved in front of her, then crouched down between her legs so their faces were only inches apart. "I'm going to look for another lump on your head. Tell me if I hurt you." His voice was low and throaty, and a stab of desire jolted through her. Her throat swelled, and all she could do was nod her head.

Griff's brown eyes held hers for a moment, and she thought she saw an answering flare of desire in their depths. Then he abruptly turned his head away. His hands slid into her hair, and she closed her eyes to the wave of feeling that swept over her.

His fingers moved gently over her scalp, probing lightly. Sensations crashed through her, making her breath catch in her chest. Blood roared in her ears, and she longed to lean into him, longed to feel the hard length of his body pressed against hers.

"Do you feel anything?" His voice sounded a little breathless.

Yes, she wanted to tell him. *You're making me feel things I've never felt before.* But instead she said, "No, I can't feel a thing."

"How about over here?" His hands drifted below her right ear, and she closed her eyes and let herself float on the sensations.

Suddenly her eyes flew open. "Ouch. That hurts." She reached up and found a tiny bump on her head.

Griff rose from between her legs and sat down on the couch next to her. Gently, he pushed the hair away from the spot. "It's a very small bump, and the skin isn't broken. They must have hit you just hard enough to make you fall down, then rolled you up in the rug. You were wriggling when they walked out the door of the apartment with you. That's when I saw one of the kidnappers hit you again.''

His fingers brushed through her hair again, and it almost felt as if he were caressing her. He leaned closer, and she thought she felt his lips brush over the spot on her head. ''It's going to be fine.''

''I didn't even know it was there until you touched it.'' Her breathing was ragged.

Griff drew away, but he didn't move off the couch. He took her hands and slowly turned her to face him. ''Do you hurt anywhere else?''

She ached all over, but that had nothing to do with her attackers. ''No, I'm fine.''

''Then I'd say you're going to survive.''

His melodic voice dropped almost to a whisper, and Willa couldn't tear her gaze away from his face. His eyes blazed with a heat she'd never seen in them before. He reached out and framed her face with his hands, then leaned toward her.

''Tell me to stop, Blue.'' His voice was a low, smoky growl that thrummed deep inside her. ''Tell me to get lost.''

Slowly she shook her head. ''I don't want you to stop,'' she whispered.

His eyes darkened and his hands slid down her neck, his thumbs tracing a line on her throat in a slow caress that made her tighten with need. Then he grasped her shoulders with shaking hands. The air between them trembled.

His kiss wasn't tender or tentative. He crushed her mouth beneath his, drinking her in like a man who'd been dying of thirst. He claimed her mouth with an untamed desperation that stirred an answering wildness in her.

Wrapping her arms around him, she pulled him closer. With a groan deep in his throat, Griff slid his hands around her face, holding her while his mouth roamed over her cheeks, her eyes, her neck.

Finally he returned to her mouth, where his lips gentled. He nibbled, he tasted, he nipped, until dark waves of heat swept over her, leaving her needy. She opened her mouth to moan his name, and he swept inside to taste her more intimately.

His hands slid down her back, caressing her spine, smoothing over every muscle along the way. Desire coiled inside her, until she throbbed in rhythm with every touch of his hands, every movement of his lips.

She tried to move closer to him. She needed to feel the hard planes of his body against hers, needed to feel his weight and heat pressing into her. His hands tightened on her for a moment, then he pressed her down onto the couch.

His leg curled around hers, and he leaned over her. His eyes were nearly black with passion, and the planes of his face were hard. "For God's sake, Willa. Tell me to stop."

She looked up at him, knowing her eyes were dazed, knowing that he could see the desire and passion in her face. "I don't want you to stop, Griff. Kiss me again."

He closed his eyes as a shudder passed through him, then he bent and took her mouth again. He smoothed her hair away from her face, and his hand trailed down her neck. He stroked the skin of her throat at the opening of her blouse, then pressed his mouth to the spot.

"You're so soft," he whispered. "So smooth. Are you this soft everywhere?"

He hesitated for a moment, then he slowly pulled her blouse out of the waistband of her slacks. He kissed her again as he slid his hand onto her abdomen.

Her skin jumped and heated at his touch, and she shifted against him. His leg slid between hers, and she pressed herself closer to him. She clung to him, lost in the sensations crashing over her. She still couldn't believe that Griff apparently wanted her as much as she wanted him.

"Griff," she said fiercely, turning so that her body fitted more closely against his.

He wove his hands into her hair, pulling her closer. His mouth took hers in a storm of heat and desire, and she answered him back, kiss for kiss, touch for touch.

But when he shifted his hand he pressed against her cut, and she couldn't stop herself from crying out. He stilled immediately, then began easing himself away from her.

"I'm sorry, Willa," he said.

"Don't be." Her voice was fierce. "You didn't mean to touch my bruise."

"That's not what I meant. I'm sorry I touched you in the first place, sorry it got out of hand."

Slowly she drew away from him, feeling a ball of hurt swelling in her throat. "You'll notice I wasn't objecting too much."

"You should have been. My God, Willa, I gave Ryan my word that I would take care of you. I promised him that I would protect you. I'm sure that what we were just doing wasn't what he had in mind."

She couldn't believe how much his words stung. "Does Ryan decide who you get involved with?" She tried to make her voice cool to hide her pain. "He doesn't run my life. What does he have to do with what goes on between us?"

"I don't answer to any man, including Ryan Fortune." He scowled at her and stood. "But I honor my word. And when I said I would protect you, I meant just that."

"I don't notice any kidnappers pounding at the door. So what are you worried about?"

Griff sighed and ran his hand through his short brown hair. "If I'm thinking about you, about how much I want to kiss you, I'm not thinking about how to protect you. My mind can't be in two places at once. And when I was kissing you, that's definitely all I was thinking about."

She angled her chin at him, unwilling to concede the point. "You said no one followed us. No one knows where we are. So what are you worried about?''

''I'm worried about what I can't predict. I'm worried about where the next threat is coming from. I had no idea that you were going to be kidnapped when I showed up at your apartment. It just happened. And I have no way of knowing what's going to happen next.''

She looked out the window at the trees surrounding the cabin and the mountain rising behind it, then looked back at Griff. His face was closed off and remote. ''What kind of man are you, Griff, that you worry about things like that?'' she asked softly.

''I'm the kind of man you don't need in your life,'' he said harshly. ''I'm the kind of man your mother should have warned you about.''

''My mother left us when I was a baby,'' she said coolly. ''So her opinion wouldn't count. And my father taught me to pay attention to my instincts. But apparently my instincts were wrong.''

''Damn right your instincts were wrong.'' He scowled again. ''I'm going out to get some firewood. It's going to get cold in here.''

Griff slammed out the door, and Willa sank back onto the couch. In spite of Griff's words, he couldn't deny what she'd seen in his face. Or felt in his touch. He had wanted her, as much as she'd wanted him.

She closed her eyes to savor the knowledge, to wrap herself in the warmth of Griff's desire for a moment longer. These last few months, when she'd been dreaming of Griff, imagining his kiss, he'd been thinking about her, too. He hadn't merely been overcome by unexpected passion. She might not be very worldly, but she could tell when a man wanted her.

And Griff had wanted her.

Logs thumped against the side of the house, jerking her back to reality. The sound reminded her that they were in this cabin because someone wanted to kidnap her, or worse. Someone hated her enough to want to harm her.

Griff was right, she told herself. She should be worrying about what had brought them here, not about Griff and how he felt about her. Or how she felt about him.

Griff wouldn't fit into her life. He would never want to settle down in a university town like College Station. She couldn't imagine him as the husband of a college professor, going to faculty dinners and cocktail parties. She couldn't imagine him as a husband, period. Griff was too wild, too untamed to fit into an easy, comfortable life-style like the one she was building.

A small voice in the back of her brain pointed out that being a college professor, having a stable and secure life, was her father's dream for her. It hadn't always been *her* dream. But she banished the voice from her mind. Being a college professor was the life she'd chosen, and she was damn good at it. And she would go on being good at it, as soon as they figured out who wanted to kidnap her.

In the meantime, she'd stay as far away from Griff as possible. It wasn't going to be easy to avoid him in this tiny cabin, but she'd do her best. There would be no repeats of the kiss they had shared.

Griff was right. They both had other things to worry about.

She stifled her heart's protest and stood. If Griff was getting firewood, she could make lunch.

Griff raised the ax again and brought it crashing down on the log. It split into several satisfying pieces, and he bent down to stack them in the growing pile next to him.

The wood piled next to the house had needed to be split before it could be used, and Griff was happy to do the job. He figured if he raised the ax and brought it down enough times, if he pushed his body to the breaking point, he'd get rid of the desire that still pulsed inside him.

He still couldn't believe he'd kissed Willa—and that he would have done a hell of a lot more than kiss her if he hadn't accidentally touched the bruise on the side of her head.

Thank God she'd flinched. It had brought him to his senses, and not a moment too soon. He'd been so consumed with his need for her that in another few minutes he'd have had her naked underneath him on the couch.

He cringed when he thought about it. He was here to protect Willa, to make sure that nothing happened to her. And the first time they were alone together, he had forgotten everything he'd been trained to remember.

Some protector *he* was.

He swung the ax again and split apart another log. At the rate he was going, he thought sourly, he'd have the whole forest split and stacked before his desire for Willa disappeared.

Why couldn't Willa have been a woman from his world, one who knew the rules and how the game was played? Why couldn't she have been the kind of woman who could indulge in a casual affair and then walk away with no regrets?

Willa *wasn't* that kind of woman. She was a lady— a college professor, for God's sake. He was the last man she should get involved with. He was too cynical, too wild, too much a loner for a woman like Willa. She needed someone who could give her what she deserved: a home, the picket fence around it, and everything that went inside.

All the things that he couldn't give her.

Why would she want to get involved with someone like him, someone who dealt in death and destruction? If she knew the real Griffin Fortune, she would run away as fast as she could.

So, they would have to get through this enforced isolation together and hope that Ryan uncovered some information—and quickly. He'd call Ryan tonight, he thought, and let him know that they'd arrived.

And make sure Ryan worked fast.

The fire in the huge fireplace crackled in front of them, radiating heat throughout the room. Griff picked up the poker and stirred the fire again. It didn't need stirring, but it was better than the alternative, which was watching Willa.

"Tomorrow I'll figure out how to turn on the heat in the cabin," he said.

Willa looked up from the book she was reading. "Don't worry about it. The fireplace keeps the cabin plenty warm. And with any luck, we won't be here too much longer."

Her voice was cool and polite, and her eyes were guarded.

When he'd finally gone back into the cabin after chopping the wood, he had found that she'd made lunch. She'd smiled at him and they'd talked, but her eyes had been wary and her words had been careful.

It was just as well. They'd both be happier in the long run if they ignored the heat that flared between them. Neither of them needed the tension that hummed in the room. And they didn't need a repeat of that kiss they'd shared.

But her taste, the way she felt, was burned into his mind. It would be a long, long time before he forgot about Willa.

"I'm going to call Ryan tonight, anyway," he said, looking at the fire again. It was too painful to look at Willa and know she was out of his league. "I'll ask him about the heat. It was easy enough to turn on the water. I'm sure the heat will be simple, too."

"Fine," she said, her tone of voice implying that she didn't care. "But don't worry about it because of me."

"You're tough, right? You can survive in near-freezing temperatures?"

She looked up at the savage tone of his voice. "It's not anywhere close to freezing. The temperature in the cabin has been very pleasant." Her voice was logical and even.

"It's the middle of December, Willa. We're in the mountains. It gets cold. It might even snow." He was taking out his frustration on her, but he couldn't stop himself.

"If it does, we'll turn on the heat." She gave him a calm smile, and added, "Do you need some help splitting the wood? I can do that, too."

"I do not need help splitting the wood." He forced himself to speak slowly and distinctly. What he wanted to do was yell at Willa, tell her that there was no way he was risking letting her use an ax.

He jumped up in disgust and stormed to the window. What he really wanted to do was sweep Willa into his arms and savor another taste of her. Only this time it would be more intense, because he knew how quickly she responded. And he knew that she wanted him, too.

The fact that Willa seemed oblivious to the tension and the desire that threatened to spill out was infuriating. But he knew better than to let it provoke him. So he strode over to the counter and picked up the phone. "I'm going to call Ryan and let him know we arrived. He might have some information for us."

Her eyes became animated for the first time since

he'd come back into the cabin. "Maybe the kidnappers have already been caught."

"Maybe." He doubted it. They had too little information to work with. "You'll be glad to get back to College Station, won't you?"

Her eyes became cool again. "I'm sure you'll be glad to get back to your own life. You can't enjoy baby-sitting me."

She had no idea how much he'd enjoyed taking care of her that afternoon. He scowled at her. "Both of us have things to do, I guess. Let me see if Ryan is around."

He dialed the private number for Ryan's office, and his uncle picked up on the first ring. "Fortune here."

"Ryan, this is Griff. I wanted to let you know that we arrived safely."

"Good." He heard the older man take a deep breath. "Lily and I have both been worried sick all day. I'm glad you called."

"We picked up enough supplies to last awhile, and no one followed us here. So we should be safe. Have you heard anything from College Station?"

"Not a thing." Griff could practically hear Ryan frown. "I have a team of the best investigators in College Station working on the case, and none of them have been able to come up with even a hint of a lead. There's no trace of the blue van. Apparently it vanished into thin air. And the management of Willa's apartment building says they didn't hire any painters or any carpet layers. There wasn't supposed to be anyone in that building when she arrived home.''

"So they were waiting specifically for her." Griff felt a coldness squeeze his gut.

"That would be my guess. The only question is why."

"I'm figuring it has something to do with you. Maybe they thought they could get ransom money out of you. Maybe it's someone with a grudge. Someone like Cling Lockhart."

There was silence on the other end of the line. "I've thought about that," Ryan said finally, reluctantly. "And we both know what he's capable of. Until we catch the culprits, take care of Willa. I think you'll be safe where you are. Don't take any chances with her. Or yourself."

"Don't worry. I know what I'm doing."

"That's why I'm not worrying."

Griff asked a few more questions about the cabin, and received instructions for turning on the heat and several other maintenance problems. He finally asked if he wanted to talk to Willa.

"Just give her my love," Ryan said.

Reassured that Ryan was taking the threat seriously, Griff said goodbye, telling Ryan he'd talk to him again soon.

When he walked back into the main room, Willa watched him with wary eyes. "What did Ryan have to say?" she asked.

"They haven't found anything. Not a trace of the van, not a trace of the housepainters. According to the management of your building, there were no painters or carpet layers scheduled to work that day.''

"So what do we do now?'' she said, licking her lips.

He turned away abruptly as desire sharpened inside him. "We wait. Ryan has hired the best investigators in College Station. Sooner or later, our kidnappers will make a mistake. Then we'll have them.''

"I should have asked you to let me talk to Ryan.''

Her voice sounded wistful, and he tried to push away the softening inside him. "That wouldn't have been a good idea. I didn't want to take a chance on someone overhearing your conversation. There are a lot of people in and out of Ryan's office every day.''

Her eyes widened, and a ripple of fear crossed her face. "I hadn't thought of that.''

"Don't worry about it,'' he said, cursing himself for alarming her. "We're not going to call him that often. There's not much chance anyone will be able to overhear our calls.''

Willa laid her book on the couch and stood. "How long do you think we'll be here, Griff?'' she asked quietly.

He shrugged. "I have no idea. It could be a couple of days, it could be longer than that.'' The devil that was riding him made him add, "You said it didn't matter. You said you didn't care when you got back to your classes. I believe you said something like, you'd worry about that when you had to.''

"I'm not worried about my classes. I just don't

think it's a good idea to stay here, together, for any longer than we have to."

For a moment, a shadow of the desire he'd seen in her eyes that afternoon flickered on her face, then was gone. She was trying very hard to hide her feelings for him, but Willa was a transparent woman. It was obvious that she'd had no experience hiding how she felt. And for that moment, exultation filled him.

He banished it as quickly as it appeared. "I agree. But we don't have a lot of choice right now. I'm going to bed. I didn't get a lot of sleep last night."

After checking all the windows and the door one more time, he turned and headed up to the loft.

By the time he was ready for bed, Willa had turned off the lights in the main room of the house and closed her bedroom door. There was a faint glow in the cabin, and he assumed it came from the light escaping from underneath her door.

He wouldn't think about Willa in the bedroom, he told himself. He needed to get some sleep if he was going to be any good at all the next day.

He fell asleep almost immediately, but his sleep was restless and unsettled.

He could stop himself from thinking about Willa. But he couldn't stop himself from dreaming about her.

Four

Eyes bleary and weariness dogging him, Griff dragged himself out of bed early the next morning. He didn't want to face yet another dream of Willa. So he walked noiselessly downstairs and started the coffee.

There would be no newspapers on the front porch to tell him what was going on in the world, no messages from his boss sending him to the latest global hot spot. He had a whole day in front of him to fill, and nothing to do with it but spend time with Willa.

That was a dangerous prospect after the previous night. His dreams had been far too vivid, and far too enticing. He'd have to make sure he and Willa kept busy. And away from each other.

"Good morning." Willa's voice embraced him, just as if he'd conjured her up from his dreams. He spun around to face her.

"What are you doing up so early?"

She shrugged. "I couldn't sleep. How about you?"

"I couldn't sleep, either." He wondered if dreams had disturbed her sleep as much as they'd disturbed his. "Coffee's almost ready."

"Thank goodness." She moved into the kitchen,

and he saw that she wore a robe that had been hanging in the bedroom. It was tightly closed and belted securely around her waist, but he immediately began wondering what she wore underneath—if anything.

"Aren't you going to get dressed?" he asked carefully.

She shook her head. "I thought I'd have something to eat, then take a shower. If you don't mind, that is."

Hell, yes, he minded, he wanted to shout at her. She wasn't wearing her glasses, and her blue-gray eyes were huge and soft in her face. Her hair was tousled and curled wildly around her face. The damn robe outlined her curves perfectly, firing his already overheated imagination. She looked like she'd just stepped out of his dreams and into the kitchen. He wanted to reach out and fold her into his arms. Instead he shoved his hands into the pockets of his jeans.

"I guess there's no hurry. Neither of us has to rush off to work."

She smiled at him and reached for the coffeepot. "Work or not, I have to have my coffee." She poured him a cup, then took out the cream and set it on the table in front of him. "I'll get the sugar."

"You remember how I take my coffee?"

She turned away to reach into a cabinet, but not before he'd seen the slight blush on her cheeks. "My father entertained his army buddies a lot. I learned to remember what they all liked to drink. It's just a habit, I guess."

He was irritated with the disappointment he felt.

Did he want her to say that she'd studied him, that she knew all kinds of things about him?

"There's a radio in the living room," he said, trying to ignore the automatic 'yes' that sprang into his mind. "Do you want to listen to the news?"

She nodded. "I'd like to, yes. I teach political science." She gave him a quick, nervous smile. "I guess I'm a news junkie."

He hurried over to the radio, fiddling with the tuner until he found an El Paso news station with clear reception. He needed something to keep his mind off Willa. Only a saint could look at her in that bathrobe and not want to peel it away from her.

And he was far from a saint.

She didn't meet his eyes while they ate breakfast. She seemed engrossed in the news from the radio, half turning to hear it. While she wasn't facing him, Griff devoured her with his eyes.

When the news was interrupted by a commercial, she turned back to face him. She went very still, and he saw her eyes darken. Her breath caught in her throat, and he knew she had seen the need in his face.

"I'm going to take a shower and get dressed," she said, standing up too quickly. The chair toppled over and fell to the floor with a crash. "Sorry. I'll clean the dishes when I'm finished."

She backed up a few steps, then turned and hurried into the bedroom. She was smart to run away, he thought as the door closed behind her. Because he was finding it harder and harder to control himself. He, who had always prided himself on his control, who had always before had the ability to walk away, was having a very hard time putting Willa out of his mind.

It was just the circumstances, he tried to tell himself. They were alone in this cabin, and might be for a while. She was in danger, and he had vowed to protect her. He hadn't had nearly enough sleep in the last two days. Of course his groggy mind would try to build his attraction to Willa into something more than it was.

It was only hormones and the scent of danger. He'd seen it often enough in his line of work. He worked for the British government. He was what the romantic Americans would call a spy, but all that meant was that he did the dirty jobs no one else would do.

Willa would probably be horrified if she knew the person he really was. She was grateful to him, and he had been too long without a woman. That's all there was to it.

Telling himself that the explanation satisfied him, he began to clear the table. When he found himself hoping that it took Willa a long time to shower and dress, he slammed the dishes down on the counter. This was going to be a hell of a long day.

By the time Willa emerged from the bedroom, Griff had settled in the living room. He was still listening to the radio, with the appearance of complete attention. But she noticed that he tensed as soon as the door opened.

"You didn't have to clean up the kitchen," she

said, standing behind the couch. "I said I would do it."

"There wasn't that much to do. And why should you do all the kitchen work?" His voice was surly, and he didn't turn around to face her.

"You chopped all the wood yesterday. It's only fair that I do my share of the chores."

"Fine. We'll figure out a 'fair' distribution of the work."

She moved around the couch and sat down in one of the chairs. Griff had a brooding look on his face. "What's wrong?" she asked softly. The anger that had stirred in her at the sound of his sharp voice a moment ago disappeared completely. Something was bothering him.

She didn't think he was going to answer, because he stared into the fireplace for a long time.

Then he sighed. "I'm not used to just sitting and waiting. I need to do something. I want to be in College Station, hunting for those kidnappers."

She scooted over to sit on the edge of the chair, and took hold of her courage. "I'm glad you mentioned that. I was thinking the same thing."

"What do you mean?" He gave her a suspicious look.

"I don't want to just sit here, either. I think we should go back to College Station."

His eyebrows came together in a frown. "Why would we want to do that? That's where the kidnappers are, presumably. That's why we left. Why would I take you back there?"

"You just said you wanted to do something. Well, so do I. If we go back to College Station, maybe we can lure them out into the open. I'll go into my office at the university, do my usual chores and just generally make myself visible. Then when they try to kidnap me again, we can catch them." She beamed at him. "What do you think?"

"I think you're crazy, that's what I think." He shot up from the couch and paced over to the window, then he turned and gave her an incredulous look. "What makes you think I would do something as insane as that?"

"It makes a lot of sense." She raised her chin. "What if the kidnappers just sit and wait until I'm back in College Station? Ryan's investigators will never find them. We'll be stuck in this cabin for ages, and when I finally go back to my job, they'll just wait for a chance to grab me again."

"Then we'll stay here until they're caught."

She saw the flashes of anger in his eyes, but she refused to back down. They'd only been at the cabin a day, but already the tension in the air was disturbing her sleep and making her jittery. "That might not be possible, Griff, and you know it. We don't really know anything about the kidnappers. How can we find them unless we have more information about them? At least if I'm in College Station, we can hope they make another kidnapping attempt."

"So you want to become bait?" His eyes flashed at her. "You want to go home and walk around with a target on your back? You want to spend all your time wondering if today is going to be the day? And what if they only want to kill you? What then? Maybe they won't even try to kidnap you again. Maybe there'll just be a sniper shot, and you won't even know what hit you. Have you forgotten my sister Matilda getting shot at on her honeymoon?''

The fury in his eyes would have made most people retreat, but she stood her ground. ''Of course I haven't forgotten, and I thank God she's okay. But if they'd wanted to kill me, they could have done that in the hall of my apartment building. Besides, how else are we going to catch them?''

The anger faded as she watched him, and he finally sighed. Running his fingers through his hair, he said, ''That's not an option, Willa. I won't put you in that kind of danger. Forget about it.''

''Who gave you the right to decide what I would and wouldn't do?'' She took a step toward him, feeling her own anger grow. ''I'm not a child, Griff. You can't tell me to stay here like a good little girl while the grown-ups take care of me.'' She moved closer to him and poked a finger at his chest. ''You may be used to telling your sister how to live, but this is *my* life we're talking about. I'm not going to let you decide how I deal with this.''

A heat that wasn't anger flared in his eyes, and his hand closed around hers, trapping it against his chest. ''No, you're not a little girl, Willa,'' he almost growled. ''I'm far too aware of that. But just because I'm attracted to you doesn't mean we're going to turn tail and run back to College Station.''

His heart pounded beneath her hand, and her breath felt as if it were caught in her throat. "You're attracted to me?" she asked, and to her disgust her voice squeaked with surprise.

He stared at her, and she saw raw, naked need in his eyes. It was the kind of need that Willa Simms had never stirred in a man before, at least not a man like Griffin Fortune. He was a man who could have anyone he chose. He probably had women throwing themselves at him. But apparently he wanted her—quiet, ordinary-looking, studious Willa.

Her heart soared and an answering need stirred deep inside her. Then Griff stepped away, letting go of her hand. He let her fingers slide through his slowly, then he shoved his hands into his pockets.

"Oh, yeah, I'm attracted to you," he said, his voice harsh and rough. "But I know that you come from a different world from mine. I know we have nothing in common. Don't worry, it's not going to interfere with what I have to do—which is protect you. And we're *not* going back to College Station."

"I still think it's the right thing to do." She spoke quietly as she turned away from him. He was right. He might be attracted to her—and God knew she was attracted to him—but their lives couldn't be following more different paths. So the smart thing to do was ignore that attraction and try to focus on why they were here in El Paso. "How are we going to catch the kidnappers if they don't know where we are?"

"That's not our concern right now."

She could feel him close behind her, but she

wouldn't turn around. She couldn't. She suspected that he would have no trouble reading her face right now. And she didn't want to be the pathetic spinster who was panting after a man she couldn't have.

"That's exactly our concern right now," she forced herself to say.

"How would your godfather feel if you got hurt?" he said, laying his hands on her shoulders. He squeezed once, then let her go. "You know how much Ryan cares about you."

"I know," she whispered, longing for him to touch her again. "He's been so good to me."

"Then do him a favor and stay here, where you'll be safe. Don't make him worry about you, too."

She spun around to face him, but there was only understanding in his eyes. "You're not playing fair," she said.

He nodded. "I know. But that doesn't change anything. Ryan and Lily would both be sick with worry if you went back to College Station. Give your godfather a little time. If he hasn't found something by the time you have to start teaching again, we'll discuss going back to College Station."

"That's weeks away," she said, appalled.

"I'm sure Ryan's investigators will come up with something before then."

He moved several steps away from her, as if he needed some distance, and said, "I'd like to check out the area today. How do you feel? Are you up to a hike?"

She touched the cut on her head. It no longer

throbbed, but it was still a little sore. "I'd love to go for a hike. My head is fine."

"We're at a higher elevation here than in College Station," he warned. "You have to worry about altitude sickness as well as your injury. Promise me that if your head starts to hurt or if you get light-headed at all, you'll tell me."

"I promise, Griff." She turned to grab her coat. "Believe me, I'm not a martyr."

"I hope not," he muttered. "Let's go, then."

"I'm ready." She stuffed her hat and gloves into her pocket, and followed him out the door.

"Hold on a minute," he said, and he turned back to the door.

"What are you doing?"

He tossed her a grim look over his shoulder. "Just setting a few traps so I can check for uninvited visitors when we get back here. I'll want to know if anyone's been in the house."

The sun was warm on her back, but Willa felt a chill as she watched Griff. His world *was* very different from hers, she acknowledged. In her world, she didn't worry about dangerous people waiting in ambush for her inside her own house. She didn't think about escape routes, as Griff was doing now. She watched his gaze linger on the shed where his truck was hidden, then scan the road and the area around the house.

She shivered, then wrapped her arms around herself. Finally Griff walked over to her. "It looks like you're cold. Do you want to wait until it warms up a bit?''

"I'm fine," she said. "I'll warm up as soon as we start walking."

"Let's go, then," he said. He hoisted the backpack he'd had in the trunk onto his shoulders and led the way out of the clearing surrounding the cabin.

The mountain rose behind the circle of trees that ringed the house, but there was a path that seemed to lead through the boulders and the bushes. Griff started out on it, then turned and waited for her to catch up with him.

"How are you doing?"

"I'm doing great," she said. And she was. The winter air was crisp and clean, and felt fresh on her tongue. "This was a good idea."

He gave her a nod, but she saw the warm approval in his eyes. She would keep up with him no matter what, she vowed.

They hiked steadily upward as the sun rose in the sky, warming her and the rocks that surrounded them. She unbuttoned her jacket and finally took it off, wrapping it around her waist. Griff maintained an even pace as they moved up the mountain. She managed to keep up with him, but she wished she'd spent more time at the health club in the last few months. Griff had been right. The air was thinner here in the mountains, and she was already breathing more heavily.

"We're about halfway to the top of this peak," he

said, glancing over his shoulder at her. "Let's stop here for a while."

"We can go as high as you like," she said, struggling not to pant. "I'm doing fine."

He stepped off the path and pulled her down onto a large boulder. "You're doing great. You must be in wonderful shape." He hadn't let go of her hand, and he absently rubbed it between both of his. "I stopped because we both need to go more slowly than usual until we get used to the altitude."

It felt to her as if sparks flew off her hand as he continued to caress it, but he didn't seem to notice. She struggled to catch her breath, but she suspected that the altitude had nothing to do with her sudden difficulty breathing. Griff's closeness and the way he was touching her were responsible.

"Did you have a particular reason for coming up here?" she finally asked.

He shrugged and leaned forward, trapping her hand between his knees. "I just wanted to get a look at the area. It's always smart to know where you are and what's around you."

"As in, looking for an escape route?"

He shot her a quick glance, and she thought there was admiration in his eyes. "You figure things out quickly."

"It wasn't that tough," she answered, her voice dry. "After watching you set all your little traps before we left the cabin this morning, it wasn't a big leap to realize you wanted to figure out a route away from the cabin."

"You never know when we'll need to have a way out." He looked away from her, and she saw his gaze scan the horizon. "You always want to have a back door."

"And what's our back door in this case?" She tried to keep her voice light, but she knew that Griff was telling her something important. He would always have a back door, in every aspect of his life. He had probably been able to slip away from every woman who had fallen for him over the years—using one of his back doors.

She eased her hand away from his and curled it into her lap. She told herself she was doing the smart thing, but she suddenly felt much colder.

"There's only the one road," he said slowly, pointing to the narrow dirt track they'd taken to the cabin. "So we couldn't drive out any other way. But there's always this pile of rocks. As a last resort, they could hide you for a while. Especially at night."

He turned to face her. "Remember that, Willa. If something happens in the cabin, don't get in the car and start driving. Run out here instead, and hide until you can get a good look around. Don't leave the area until you're sure that there isn't anyone waiting for you on the road."

She shivered in spite of the warm sun on her back. "Nothing is going to happen at the cabin," she said, her voice insistent. "No one aside from Ryan knows where we are. There's no way anyone could find us."

"I hope to God that's true." His voice was sober,

and he looked around broodingly. "But don't forget about this back door, and use it if you have to."

"You're giving me the creeps," she said, and she stood. "Let's check out the view from the top of this pile of rocks."

He stood too, but didn't start walking. "Maybe we've done enough for one day. Are you sure you want to keep going?"

"Of course I want to keep going. We might find another one of your back doors from the top of this hill."

"All right, but we'll take it nice and slow. I don't want you falling on your bum when I'm not looking."

"Don't worry. I'll give you plenty of warning if I'm going to fall."

He looked over his shoulder to give her a grin, and it stole her breath away. "You've got a sassy mouth on you, Willa Simms. Are all American women like you?"

"I don't know," she said, willing her racing heart to slow down. "Are all Aussie men dark and brooding and wild?"

He grinned at her again. "They'd like to think so. But most of them are like my brothers, upstanding citizens and all-around good guys."

"Don't you belong in that category, too?" she asked.

His grin disappeared. "No one is ever going to call me an upstanding citizen, let alone a good guy."

"I don't know," she said quietly. "I think you're a pretty good guy."

He didn't answer, but she knew he had heard her, because his shoulders tightened. After a long time, he said, "Don't wear those rose-colored glasses when you look at me, Willa. I'm not one of the good guys."

"If you weren't one of the good guys, you wouldn't be here with me."

"I'm here with you precisely because I'm *not* a good guy. Why do you think Ryan asked me to check on you and look at your security system? It was because I know far more than any good guy ever will about the bad things that can happen to people."

"I've heard the rumors about what you do for a living. Are they true?"

He turned to give her a smile, but there wasn't an ounce of humor in the grim curve of his lips. "I'm sure none of them are true. People like you and the Fortunes can't imagine the kind of things I do. You're all far too nice to visualize my world."

"If that's true, it just makes you more willing than most of us to do what needs to be done. And makes you more of a good guy than I thought."

He shook his head, weariness in his eyes. "Don't be naive, Willa. No one does what I do, day after day, year after year, without having it stain his soul. Believe me, there's nothing noble about what I do. And not even your American optimism can make it so."

"Don't sell yourself short, Griff," she answered quietly. "And don't even bother trying to convince me that you're the devil incarnate. It won't work."

"Suit yourself," he said with a shrug, turning away

from her and walking more quickly up the trail. "But don't be surprised when your pet dog turns and bites you."

"You're not going to hurt me," she said, hurrying to keep up with him. "And nothing you can say will make me believe that you would."

He didn't answer, and they hiked in silence for a while, walking steadily uphill. Willa realized she was beginning to gasp for breath. They weren't that high—the mountains around El Paso ranged from 4,000 to about 7,000 feet. But for someone used to living at close to sea level, that was a big difference.

She was just about to ask Griff to slow down, when they reached the top of the hill. Griff stood in front of her for a moment, turning slowly to take in the view, then he looked at her.

"Pretty spectacular," he said, his voice impersonal. It was as if their conversation of a few minutes ago had never taken place.

"It's magnificent." She turned slowly, ignoring Griff, just drinking in the sight. Miles and miles of Texas and Mexico unfolded in front of them, mountain peaks rising, purple and red, from the barren-looking, dun-colored desert, which was only interrupted by scattered patches of dark green. "It's certainly worth the hike."

She turned and peered down in the direction of the cabin. "Look, you can barely see the cabin. It almost looks swallowed by the trees around it."

"Are you feeling all right?" he asked gruffly.

She looked over at him with surprise. "I'm fine. Why?"

"I should have gone more slowly up this last part of the trail. You can't be used to hiking at this altitude."

"I'm fine," she said again, vowing she wouldn't say anything that would give away the fact that a headache was beginning to throb beneath her temples. She was tired of feeling like an invalid. She'd only gotten a small bump on the head, for crying out loud. Griff was acting as if she'd practically been bludgeoned senseless.

"Let's sit down and eat something."

Her stomach rolled once at the thought of food, but she sat down. "I didn't realize you'd put anything into that pack of yours."

"I didn't. I always carry some nuts or candy and water in my pack." He stared at her with a challenge in his eyes. "I never know when I'll get stuck in a tight spot and need it."

"Thank goodness for that. I'm getting a little thirsty."

He passed her water in a plastic bottle, and she drank it down. Setting the empty bottle on the rock beside her, she looked at it, amazed. "I didn't realize I was *that* thirsty."

"This altitude can dehydrate you pretty quickly." His gaze searched her face. "Are you light-headed at all?"

"Not a bit," she lied. In fact, her head was beginning to feel detached from her body. "If I sit here for a few minutes and catch my breath, I'll be ready to start back down the trail.''

Griff tried to hand her a candy bar, but she shook her head. ''No, thanks. I'm not hungry.''

He gave her a searching look, but didn't say anything. Eating his own candy bar slowly, he drank some of his water, then passed her the bottle.

She eyed it longingly, but shook her head. ''I've had my fill.'' She wasn't about to take water away from Griff. He was bigger than she was, and he undoubtedly needed more.

''Are you sure?''

''Positive,'' she said firmly. It wouldn't take nearly as long to get back down the mountain. Then she could have as much water as she wanted.

They sat quietly for a while, and eventually her breathing sounded less raspy and strained. Her head still ached, but she was determined to ignore it. When Griff said, ''Ready to go?'' she nodded.

Griff led the way again, and she followed him down the trail. Her shoes caught on a loose rock, and she slid for a foot or so. Catching herself on a boulder alongside the trail, she looked up to find Griff beside her.

''Are you all right?''

''I just slipped on a rock,'' she said, holding onto him as the world spun slowly around her. ''I'll watch where I'm going.''

He stood and looked at her, and she could see the worry in his eyes. ''I think we came too far up,'' he said finally.

"Don't be silly," she replied, standing and pulling her jacket more tightly around her waist. "I'm fine."

But as she began to walk again, they rounded a turn in the trail. Instead of following the curve, she stepped off the edge of the trail—and into the air.

Five

Griff heard the clatter of rocks behind him and was spinning around even before he heard Willa's high-pitched, terrified scream. She tumbled over the edge of the trail and seemed to fall in slow motion away from him. He grabbed for her arm, and fell onto the rocks, but she was gone before he could catch her.

"Willa?" he called, holding his breath to hear her voice.

"I'm okay, I think." Her voice came from below him, and although it was shaky, it sounded damn wonderful.

Afraid that the edge of the trail had crumbled and broken off, he wriggled over to the drop-off on his stomach. Willa had landed on a small ledge about ten feet below him. She sat there, a bewildered look on her face, and stared up at him.

"Are you hurt?" he asked, his voice sharp.

"I don't think so." He could see her move her legs and feet. "Everything seems to be working."

"What happened? Did the rock crumble on the trail?"

She shifted her gaze away from him. "I don't think so."

"Then how did you fall?"

"I just fell," she said, but she still wouldn't look up at him.

"Willa, something's wrong." His voice sharpened even more, and he swung his leg over the side of the small cliff. "I'm coming down there."

"Don't," she said, finally looking at him. "I know what's wrong. I let myself get light-headed and dizzy from the altitude and didn't say anything to you. Okay? Are you satisfied?"

Her voice sounded belligerent, but he could see the flags of color on her cheeks and the embarrassment in her eyes, even from this distance.

"All right," he said, and made his voice soothing. "Let's not worry about why it happened. Let's get you off that little ledge."

He opened his pack to remove the small coil of rope he stored there, praying that it would be strong enough to lift Willa. He didn't like the look of that small outcropping of rock. The rock around him was soft and crumbling, and all he could see in his mind's eye was the ledge giving way and Willa falling endlessly away from him.

The rope was just long enough to reach to the ledge and Willa. "Can you tie this around your waist?" he called, keeping his voice calm and even.

"I think so."

"Do you know how to tie a bowline knot?"

"No." She looked up at him. "But if you talk me through it, I'm sure I could learn."

They didn't have time for Willa to learn how to tie

the complicated knot. As she shifted on the ledge to loop the rope around her waist, a small piece of the rock flaked off and fell. It was a long time before he heard it hit on the boulders below.

"Don't worry about it. Just tie a square knot. You can do that, can't you?"

"I'm not an idiot," she snapped, and he relaxed slightly. If she could snap at him, she couldn't be hurt too badly.

"All right," she called after a few moments. "I've got the rope tied."

Griff tied the other end around his own waist, then looked around for something to use to brace himself. There was a tiny mesquite bush on the other side of the trail. It was pitifully small, but it would have to do. Wrapping his legs around the thin trunk, he pulled up the slack in the rope.

"I'm going to pull you slowly up the side of the cliff," he called to Willa. "All you need to do is walk up the rocks. Can you do that?"

"Yes," she called. He heard the fear in her voice.

"Let me know when you're ready."

"I'm ready."

He began to pull, slowly but steadily. The rope vibrated in his hands as Willa banged against the rocks. He could hear her panting and cursing under her breath, but she didn't ask him to stop, didn't beg for him to go more slowly. She just kept scrabbling against the rocks as he pulled her upward.

When he saw the top of her head at the edge of the

cliff, he gave a hard pull, and she slid over the edge. She lay face down on the trail and didn't move.

His heart pounding in his chest, he untangled himself from the mesquite bush and scrambled to get to her. Had she hurt herself on the ascent? Had she banged her head again?

Just as he reached her, she turned her head and gave him a wobbly smile. "Nice job, Fortune."

"My God, Willa. Are you hurt?"

She shook her head and gathered herself to sit up. "Only my pride."

He couldn't stop himself. Before he could think about what he was doing, before he could tell himself to be smart, he'd snatched her up into his arms and pulled her against him.

"I'm so sorry," he whispered into her hair, holding her more tightly.

She pulled away far enough to look at him. "What on earth are you sorry for?"

"For taking you up this damn mountain. I knew you'd had a knock on the head yesterday. I should have kept you in the cabin."

"The fact that I fell off the cliff was not your fault," she said firmly. "It's my own stupidity and pride that are to blame. I'm the one who ignored the symptoms of altitude sickness and insisted on going on. I was feeling light-headed even before we got to the top of the mountain. So don't blame yourself."

He couldn't let her go, not yet. "Why didn't you tell me you were feeling light-headed? Why didn't you tell me you needed to go back?"

"Because I didn't want you to think I was a weak, needy woman," she said, and the disgust in her voice almost made him smile. "Because I thought I could tough it out until we got back to the cabin. Instead, I endangered us both."

He pulled her against him again, and instead of trying to get away, she snuggled closer. "I don't think of you as a weak and needy woman. In fact, you're so strong that you terrify me. I'm not sure you need me at all. I think you can do anything you set your mind to, Willa."

"I wish that were true," she murmured against his chest.

"Tell me one thing you want to do that you can't do," he demanded.

When she didn't answer, he looked down at her. She looked steadily back, although the red flags were waving in her cheeks again. And beneath the embarrassment, he saw need in her eyes. Need for him, he realized, and he felt as if he'd taken a gut punch.

"What is it that you want to do?" he whispered. He knew he should back away, knew he should let go of her, but he couldn't do it.

He didn't think she was going to answer, but she leaned closer to him. "I want to kiss you," she said, her voice soft as the delicate breeze that caressed his face.

He held her gaze steadily as she leaned closer to him. Her face flamed, but she didn't stop. When she brushed his mouth with hers, his whole body clenched with desire.

She would have backed away after that one slight touch of her mouth, but he wouldn't let her go. Framing her face with his hands, he took her mouth again. This time, he wanted to taste her. This time, he wanted to feel her need growing inside her, to know that she wanted him as much as he wanted her. This time, he wanted to wrap himself around her and hold on tight.

He was making a mistake, a distant voice tried to warn him. He was going down a path he would regret taking, making choices that would come back to haunt him, but he didn't care. His need for Willa had been growing since the first time he'd seen her, and the last two days with her had only intensified his desire. The kiss they'd shared the night before had only made it worse. Now he knew what she tasted like, what she felt like.

He plunged into her, ravaging her mouth, letting the sweetness of her seep into him and fill him. Willa was everything good, everything sweet and pure. She was everything that was missing from his life. And in his desperation to taste more of her, to take more of her, he pressed her back onto the ground and held her head steady with his hand while he plundered her mouth.

''Griff,'' she gasped, clutching the sleeves of his shirt.

He jerked as if she'd hit him. She should have, he told himself savagely. He'd been on her like a rutting beast. But when he tried to ease away from her, she wouldn't let him. Her arms curled around his neck, and she pulled him back down to her.

"Don't stop," she whispered, and he felt as if someone had cracked his heart wide open. "Kiss me again, Griff."

"You don't know what you're asking," he managed to say.

Her lashes fluttered open, and her blue-gray eyes were unfocused and smoky with desire. "Then show me," she said.

He groaned and pulled her close again. It was just the fear, he told himself. That was why he couldn't resist her. She'd scared him half to death. He'd thought she had fallen to her death, and kissing her was just a reaction.

But it felt like a whole lot more than a reaction. It felt as if he'd come home, as if he'd finally found the place where he belonged. He didn't want to let Willa go, and when he finally realized that, he eased her away from him and let his arms drop to his sides.

"We need to get back to the cabin," he said, his voice still hoarse with desire. "You took a nasty fall."

He heard her make a small sound of denial in the back of her throat, and that instinctive protest almost did him in. He almost reached for her again, but instead he moved far enough away that he couldn't touch her.

"Do you think you can stand?" he asked.

She opened her eyes slowly and looked at him. The flush of passion was still on her face, and her eyes were dreamy and soft. Griff looked away before he could grab her again. Willa wasn't for him. Passion might arc between them, but that was all it could ever be.. And Willa wasn't the kind of woman who indulged in casual affairs. Willa was a happily-ever-after kind of woman. She was the kind of woman he always avoided.

"Do you want me to carry you back to the cabin?" he asked, hoping her answer would be no. He couldn't afford to touch her right now. If he did, all his good intentions would vanish like smoke in the air.

She managed to shake her head. A part of him regretted it, but as he watched her eyes clear, he told himself it was the right thing to do.

"I can walk," she said.

"I'm going to help you up," he said carefully. "Ready?"

She started to get to her feet, putting one hand out to brace herself. When she winced, he slid his hands under her arms and lifted her to her feet. He let her go so quickly that she stumbled.

"What's wrong with your hand? It's bleeding."

She glanced down at it, then clenched her fingers in her palm. "Nothing. I just scraped it on the rocks, I guess."

"We need to get you back down to the cabin," he said, and he knew his voice was rough. "Are you sure you can walk?"

"I'm sure." Her voice was stronger, and the dreaminess had faded from her eyes. Now they looked at him with a cool assurance. "I promise I'll tell you if I'm feeling light-headed again."

He could see the hurt lingering beneath the cool look, and he cursed himself for losing control, for putting that look in her eyes. "Are you upset that I kissed you, or upset that I stopped?"

"What makes you think I'm upset at all?" This time there was frost in her voice.

"You're not that hard to read, Willa."

"Really? In that case, read *this*." She pushed past him and began walking down the path in the direction of the cabin.

He watched her for a moment, surprised and awed at the strength of her will, then scrambled to catch up with her.

"Why don't we take a break?" he said gently. "You need a chance to settle down after your fall." He shoved his hands in his pockets to keep himself from touching her.

"I feel fine." She kept walking.

"I know you're tough, Willa. I know you can make it back to the cabin on your own. You don't have to prove anything to me."

Finally she stopped and turned to look at him. "I'm not trying to prove anything. I'm ashamed of myself, and that's why I want to get back to the cabin. I know I should have told you that I was having problems. I'm sorry that I endangered you, too. All right?" Her words were formal and distant.

"It's okay, Willa." He reached out to bridge the distance, cupping her cheek in his hand. "I understand. And it's not as if I've never done anything foolish. Don't worry about it.''

For just a moment, she pressed her face into his hand. But before he could react, she stepped away from him. He ached to reach out and touch her again, so he made a fist and shoved it behind his back. ''Sit down for a moment. I never had a chance to make sure you weren't hurt after your fall.''

''I think it's pretty obvious that I'm not hurt. I sure wasn't too worried about it after you rescued me.'' She lifted her head and stared at him, and beneath the defiance he could see that the emotional hurt still lingered. ''I'm sorry I asked you to kiss me. It won't happen again.''

''You think that bothered me?''

She gave him a tight-lipped smile. ''Clearly it did, since you were in such a hurry to get away from me. Don't worry, Griff. I know how you feel, and I'll respect that.''

''You have no idea how I feel,'' he muttered.

''I think I do.'' She turned away and started down the path again. ''I've had enough of a break. Let's get back to the cabin.''

Willa walked down the trail, too conscious of Griff right behind her. He was so close that she could smell the faint tang of his soap, feel the heat that radiated from his body.

He was staying so close merely because he was worried about her. And that was her own fault. She couldn't believe how stupid she'd been, and how irresponsible. She'd fallen off the edge of the mountain because she'd been too proud to admit her weakness.

She deserved every single one of the bumps and bruises that she was already feeling, she thought. Her hands burned where she'd scraped them against the rocks while she scrabbled to get up the cliff. Her hip ached, her head still hurt and her shoulders felt as if she'd been tackled repeatedly. But she had no right to whine.

When they got back to the cabin, she'd lock herself in the bedroom and soak in the tub for a year or so—after she drank about a gallon of water.

"We're almost there." His voice came from right behind her, and he touched her arm. She froze.

"Can you hold on for a moment? I want to get another look at the cabin before we go back down."

She sank down onto a rock and watched as he used a pair of binoculars to study the cabin and its surroundings. Finally she asked, "How could you tell if there was something wrong from all the way up here?"

He gave her a sharp look. "How do you know I'm looking for something wrong?"

"Please, Griff," she said wearily. "Give me a little credit."

His face softened. "I give you a lot of credit, Willa. I'm just finding it a little uncanny how you're able to read me."

"You're not that hard to read, Griff," she said, quoting his words back to him.

He gave her a reluctant smile. "I deserved that, I

guess. I'm not used to having someone know in advance what I'm doing.''

"It's just the circumstances,'' she said hurriedly. God forbid he think she was making a connection with him again. ''We're thrown together, and it's hard not to notice your patterns.''

"I was hoping I didn't have any patterns,'' he said, clamping his mouth shut and staring at the cabin again.

"Everyone does,'' she said. ''They're just more noticeable in some people.''

"Now you're telling me I'm obvious?'' His reluctant smile took the sting out of his words.

She shook her head. ''Not at all. But since my life apparently depends on you, I have a lot of incentive to figure out what you're doing.''

"I didn't realize you were so observant.'' He kept his gaze on the cabin, but she felt his attention focused on her.

She shrugged. ''It was because of the way I grew up, I guess. Since my father was in the military we moved around a lot. I learned early to watch everything. I had to make new friends all the time. It's easier to fit in if you pay attention to the people around you.''

"I'll remember that,'' he murmured. He squatted down next to her. ''You ready to start walking again?''

"I'm fine. I thought we stopped because you wanted to check out the cabin.''

"That was part of it. The other part was to give

you a chance to rest. You've got to be pretty sore after that fall.''

''I can make it back to the cabin just fine,'' she said, trying not to wince as she stood. ''Does everything look clear at the cabin?''

''Everything looks just the way we left it. I'll know better when we get closer.''

They only had a few hundred feet to go, and she felt herself slipping on the loose rocks on the trail. Griff took her arm to steady her, but let her go as soon as they reached the trees that surrounded the cabin.

''I want you to stay here,'' he said in a low voice. ''Stay hidden behind the trees. Don't come out until I come to get you.''

''All right.''

He stared at her, then touched her cheek, almost as if he couldn't help himself. ''If you hear anything that makes you uneasy, or if I don't come right back, stay here. If someone besides me comes looking for you, run back up the mountain. Don't go near the truck until you're sure it's safe. The keys are behind the front left tire. Drive away, and don't stop until you get to a police station in El Paso. Go inside and call Ryan.''

''I'm not going to leave you here.''

''If someone besides me comes looking for you, there's nothing you can do for me, anyway.''

She must have looked horrified, because he gave her a tiny grin. ''That's what's called a worst-case scenario, Blue. Nobody's found us, and there's going to be nothing wrong at the cabin. But you need to know what to do, just in case.''

''I can see that worst-case scenarios are part of your pattern,'' she said tartly, to hide the fear that had swamped her. ''Are you always so optimistic?''

''Every day of my life.'' His voice was cheerful. ''That's why I'm still alive to talk about it.'' His hand closed over her shoulder, and he gave her a squeeze. ''I'll be right back. Just sit tight for a few minutes.''

He disappeared quickly and noiselessly, vanishing into the trees. Griff would be a formidable opponent, she thought to herself. And a dangerous one.

He was already proving dangerous to her heart, and to the careful plans she'd made. Since Griff had rescued her two days ago, everything else had seemed distant and irrelevant, including her teaching job in College Station and the tidy life she'd planned for herself.

The life that your father planned for you, a tiny voice reminded her.

It was what she wanted, too. Wasn't it?

She pushed the niggling doubt away. She'd worked too hard, for too long, to get this job at the university. Of course it was what she wanted! And Griff wouldn't fit in.

Before she could continue with that line of thinking, he reappeared in front of her. ''Everything is clear,'' he said, no longer talking in the muted whisper he'd used earlier. ''None of my traps was disturbed. No one's been around. No one's even been close to the cabin.''

"Great." She headed for the cabin. Griff walked along next to her. The watchful tension that had surrounded him when they'd entered the trees had vanished. Once again, he seemed at ease and relaxed.

As soon as they were inside, she poured herself a glass of water and drank it all, then poured another one. When she'd finished about half of it, she set the glass on the counter. "Much better."

Griff watched her with concern in his eyes. "How's your headache?"

She shrugged. "It's still there. I'm sure it'll go away soon."

"I'll get you some aspirin."

She nodded. "Thanks. I'm going to take a bath. I'll see you later."

"Leave that door unlocked," he said, just as she was about to close it.

She gave him a suspicious look. "Why would I want to do that?"

"I don't want to have to break the door down in case you pass out in the bathtub. Ryan probably wouldn't appreciate that."

"I'm not going to pass out in the bathtub," she snapped. She didn't want to argue with Griff. All she wanted to do was soak away some of the aches in her body, then crawl into bed.

"Just leave the door unlocked."

"Fine." She waited until he handed her the aspirin, then shut the door with a deliberate *click*, then dropped her clothes on the floor on the way to the bathroom. It was a decadent place, with windows looking out onto the mountains and a huge tub that would fit two. Willa refused to let herself think about sharing that tub with Griff. He wasn't interested, and if she were smart, she wouldn't be, either.

The water felt blissfully good on her sore muscles, and even the stinging from the scrapes on her hands couldn't take away from her pleasure. She sank into the depths of the tub, feeling the warm water easing away the worst of the aches from her arms and legs. When her arms and legs felt buttery soft and relaxed, she turned on the hot water again and watched the steam rise off the surface of the water. She closed her eyes, savoring the warmth and relaxation, and drifted off to sleep.

The knock at the door startled her, and she jumped. The water had chilled around her, and when she moved, all her muscles protested. "What?" she said, as Griff knocked again.

"Are you all right in there, Willa?"

She heard the worry in his voice. "I'm fine," she said. "I guess I fell asleep in the tub."

"Can you get out by yourself?"

"Of course I can." Did he think she was going to ask for his help? Her face burned just thinking about it.

"I'll wait here until you're out."

She wanted to tell him to go away, but knew it would be a waste of time. So she sat up in the tub and tried to pull herself out.

Vicious pain shot through her muscles, and she

couldn't stop herself from crying out. Immediately the door to the bathroom burst open, and Griff walked in.

He grabbed a towel and held it in front of her, preserving her modesty, but she still instinctively covered herself. "Get out of here!"

"You need help getting out of that tub," he said, and he sounded implacable. "Come on, Willa. I'll help you."

Humiliated and embarrassed, she allowed him to reach down and grasp her arms, lifting her out. He immediately wrapped the towel around her and stepped away.

"Thank you," she said, and she knew her voice didn't sound very gracious. "I'm sure I can manage by myself now."

"I'll be waiting for you out in the living room," he said. Then he left, pulling the door closed behind him.

Her face burned with humiliation, but she told herself to ignore it. Clearly Griff wasn't interested in her sexually. She'd better get that through her head before she made a total fool of herself.

The sun had already slipped behind the mountain outside the window, and the trees cast long shadows over the house. It was later than she'd realized, she thought as she dried herself and put on clean clothes. It had been a big mistake to fall asleep in the bathtub. Her muscles had stiffened again as the water cooled, and they protested painfully as she dressed.

When she emerged into the living room, she saw that Griff had started a fire in the fireplace. He sat on the couch, but stood when he heard her behind him. "Come here and sit down," he said, waving her toward the couch.

She walked slowly, hating the fact that her muscles were sore, hating the fact that Griff would see her weakness. But he wrapped his arm around her and eased her to a sitting position.

"You're more sore than you expected to be, aren't you?"

She nodded.

"Anytime you take a tumble like that, you're going to feel it. Even if you don't think you hurt yourself, you'll get plenty of bruises." Once she was settled, he wrapped a blanket around her. "Do you want a cup of coffee?"

"That sounds great." She watched him, puzzled. "I thought you'd be mad at me for falling off that cliff."

"I'm not mad at you, Willa." He sat down next to her. "I'm mad at myself for taking you on a hike like that. Will you forgive me?"

"There's nothing to forgive," she said gruffly. "It's my own fault that I got hurt. If I hadn't been so darned stubborn, I wouldn't have fallen in the first place."

Six

He leaned back and looked at her. "Why don't we agree to forget about it? All's well that ends well, after all."

"That's fine with me," she said, watching him carefully. "But can you do that?"

"Of course I can."

"Are you sure?" She watched him steadily. "You're pretty hard on yourself, Griff."

Instead of answering, he folded his arms across his chest and stared at her for a moment. Finally he said, "What's that supposed to mean?"

"It means what you think it means." Exasperated, she eased herself off the couch and walked over to the window, watching the dusk eating away at the light. "It means that you blame yourself far more than most people would, and that you take far more responsibility than you need to take. It means that you don't forgive yourself easily."

"I didn't realize you were a psychologist," he drawled.

She didn't turn around to face him. She'd heard the hint of fear beneath the sarcasm, and she was afraid her compassion would show on her face. That was only one of the things Griff didn't want from her.

"I've spent two whole days with you now, Griff. And as I said, I learned early in life to pay attention. You blamed yourself for not getting to my apartment earlier when I was kidnapped, and you blamed yourself for not catching the two people who tried to take me. Now you're blaming yourself because I fell off the mountain. And none of it is your fault."

"Ryan entrusted your safety to me," he said carefully. "Taking you on a hike wasn't in the best interests of your safety."

She spun around to face him. "I already told you that I knew I was having problems and didn't tell you. So how does that make it your fault?"

"I should have been able to predict what would happen."

She gave him a tired glance. "Why should you have been able to predict my foolishness? You don't know me that well, Griff."

"I know you better than you realize," he muttered.

"I doubt it." She hoped her gaze was cool. "I can see this isn't going to work. Maybe we'd better go back to College Station, after all."

"We're not allowed to have a disagreement?" he asked.

"Is that what you call it?"

Surprisingly, his mouth curled into a faint grin. "It sounds a lot more dignified than saying we're having a fight."

She found herself reluctantly smiling back at him.

"Four days ago, I wouldn't have imagined having either a fight or a disagreement with you."

"Four days ago, you were safe in your own world."

Her smile faded. "We're back at the kidnapping. And that brings us back to College Station. I'm still not convinced we shouldn't go back there."

"Come here and sit down, Willa." Griff patted the couch.

She sat down at the other end. "We've already discussed this, Griff. And I still think it's a good idea."

"I know you do." His mouth quirked up into a tiny smile again, momentarily softening his face. He looked like a man she could care about, she thought. Then she banished the idea from her mind. That way led to nothing but heartache for her, and discomfort for Griff.

"And I think the idea stinks."

His blunt words startled her. "Don't hesitate to say how you feel, Griff."

"I never have. And I know you haven't given up on this harebrained idea of yours."

He turned to face her and took her hands. Her heart lurched in her chest, but she tried to keep her face expressionless. "I don't think it's harebrained."

"You told me that Ryan is the only family you have left. Is that true?"

"No, actually, it's not. I don't have *any* real family. Ryan is my make-believe family." She smiled, although her heart wrenched. "I was an only child of an only child."

"All right, maybe the Fortunes aren't blood relations. But they consider themselves your family, don't they?"

"Yes, they do. Ryan and my father became close friends while they were in the army. Dad asked Ryan to be my godfather and we've been close ever since."

"And you consider them your family?"

"Yes, I do."

His hands shifted, and he twined his fingers with hers. She tried to ignore the pounding of her heart. "Don't you think Ryan would be upset if anything happened to you?"

"I know he would. That's the kind of person Ryan is."

"Then why would you want to go back to College Station and take that kind of chance? Why can't you let him do this for you? He's not asking for much. He's just asking for a little bit of your time."

Willa looked down at her hands, lost in Griff's much bigger ones. "When you put it that way, you make me feel small and petty."

He gave her hands a squeeze. "I don't mean to do that. The last thing anyone could call you is small or petty. Sometimes what we want to do might sound like the best plan to us, but it would hurt other people. Then we have to decide what's more important."

She looked up at him. "You know Ryan is more important to me than going back to College Station."

He nodded, but there was a light in his eyes. "I thought you would say that. So we'll stay here."

"Do you think this is the smartest thing to do?" she asked.

For a moment his eyes hardened, and she saw the warrior inside him. "If it were just me, if I didn't have to worry about someone else, I'd be back in College Station and I'd hunt those two down. But it isn't just me. I can't do what I want to do, because there's someone else I have to think about." He turned to her, and the fierce light faded from his eyes. "Making sure you're all right is far more important than my own personal satisfaction. Those two will be caught, sooner or later. And they'll be punished. I can wait."

"You're very disciplined," she murmured.

He glanced at her, then looked into the fire. "It comes with the job. If you're not disciplined, you don't last for long."

"What *is* your job, Griff?" She gathered her courage and asked him directly. "Everyone in the Fortune family has his or her theory, but none of your siblings will tell us exactly what you do."

"That's because none of them know, exactly," he said.

"Your own brothers and sister don't know what you do for a living?" She stared at him, amazed.

"It's better that they don't know."

"And why is that?"

"It's safer for them if they don't know what I do."

"And how do you prevent them from knowing what you do?"

"I don't spend much time at home. That's safer for them, too."

"So you keep yourself isolated and stay away from your family to protect them?" A warmth blossomed and swelled inside her.

"You're making this into a big deal, Willa. Believe me, it isn't."

"I think it's a very big deal," she said softly. "You must love them very much."

"They're my family," he said. She could see the truth deep in his eyes: his family was everything to him.

"I wish I had a family like that," she said, hearing the wistful note in her own voice.

"You do. The Fortunes are your family."

"It's not the same." She gave him a smile and let go of his hands. "And now we're becoming maudlin. How about I fix some spaghetti for dinner?"

"Sounds good to me." Griff sounded as eager to change the subject as she was. "Why don't I give you a hand?"

"Great." She forced herself to smile. "You can make the salad."

"I think I can handle that."

She watched as his competent hands shredded lettuce and chopped carrots. She didn't want to discuss family with Griff. He fascinated her, but they had skated uncomfortably close to discussing her own family, and she wasn't ready to do that. After her mother walked out on them, it had been only her and her father. They had been close—she would have done anything for him.

And she had, she thought. She'd let him dictate her choice of career. She'd agreed with her father when he suggested a job as a college professor, because he was gravely ill at the time and she didn't want to upset him. And it had seemed as good an idea as any back then, when she couldn't think of anything but her father.

But after only one semester at the university, she was already chafing at the bit. And the two days she'd spent with Griff made her even more unsure of what she wanted to do with the rest of her life.

She didn't have to decide that now, she told herself. In fact, it would be a pretty bad idea to make a decision like that under these circumstances. So she would put it out of her head, and concentrate on getting through the next few days with Griff, without embarrassing herself or him again.

And that was going to be harder than she could ever have imagined. She hadn't known that she could be so wildly attracted to a man. She hadn't known that she could completely melt from one kiss. And she hadn't known how painful it would be to realize that he wasn't nearly as interested in her.

Griff watched Willa as she poured the spaghetti sauce into a pan and started the water boiling, and wondered what put such sadness in her eyes. He suspected it had something to do with her family. She'd been awfully quick to change the subject.

He wanted to wrap his arms around her and comfort her. God help him, he wanted to tell her that it felt like she belonged to him. And that thought scared him more than any assassin or any thug ever could.

He wasn't the right man for Willa. Hell, he was as far from the right man as she could get. And he'd better keep that firmly in mind.

"Why don't we eat in front of the fire?" he said, keeping his voice light. "It's a shame to waste it."

"That sounds like a great idea," she said, equally lightly. "Why don't you put that salad on the coffee table, and I'll bring over the spaghetti."

"Consider it done."

He gradually relaxed as they ate, and he even managed to carry on a normal conversation with Willa. He told her about London, where he had been based, and she told him, delightedly, that she'd spent some time there with her father. When he prodded her to tell him more about her travels around the world, she happily complied. He found there were a number of places around the globe they'd both visited.

"I didn't realize your father was posted so many places outside the U.S.," he said as he carried the remains of their dinner into the kitchen.

"I've been all over the world." She leaned back on the couch and stared at the fire. "I guess that's why I'm so attached to the Fortunes. They've been the one stable thing in my life."

He joined her on the couch, sitting far enough away to avoid temptation.

"He and my father served in the army together in

Vietnam. They always made it a point to get together once or twice a year. So I grew up as a sort of honorary cousin to all Ryan's kids. We'd stay for a few days, then move on.''

''No wonder you wanted a job like the one you have,'' he said.

''What do you mean?'' She crinkled her forehead.

''Being a university professor is about as stable a job as you can get. Once you get tenure, you're there for as long as you want to be.''

She nodded. ''It's stable, all right.'' She hesitated, and he thought she was going to add something. Instead she turned to him and said, ''And how do you like traveling the world?''

He didn't want to tell her that he didn't see the pleasant side of the various parts of the world he visited. Most of the time, all he saw was the seedy, dangerous and dark parts of each country. He definitely didn't visit the tourist attractions.

''I have a job to do,'' he finally said. ''If you ask any businessperson who travels for a living, he or she would tell you the same thing. They don't see the places they visit. They just do their job and then go home.''

''Don't you ever take vacations?''

''Yeah, I take vacations. I go home to our ranch in Australia.''

''And I go to Ryan's ranch,'' she said softly. She stared at the fire. ''It sounds like we're a lot alike.''

Her words brought pleasure to him, an insidious

pleasure that threatened to worm its way into his heart. He banished it immediately.

They weren't alike in any way, shape or form, he reminded himself savagely. Willa was a lady, a woman who taught college and knew nothing of the ugly side of life.

He was a man who lived daily in the very ugliest parts of life. He was a man who knew three hundred ways to kill with his bare hands. Griff was a man who knew things no decent man would ever know. And the darkness that ran through him, that consumed him at times, was something totally alien to a woman like Willa.

Before he could think of a clever retort, a way of pointing out to Willa that they would never be at all alike, the lights flickered off in the cabin. They came back on immediately.

Willa sat up on the couch. "What happened?"

"I'm not sure." Griff automatically reached for his gun at the small of his back, then realized he wasn't wearing it. "Stay here. I'll be right back."

He took the stairs to the loft two at a time. In moments he'd strapped his gun in place, and ran back down the stairs. Willa was on the couch, staring over her shoulder at him. Her blue-gray eyes were enormous in her face.

"Is something wrong?" Her voice was hushed.

"I don't know. But I'm not going to take any chances."

He heard her gasp as she spotted the gun at his back, but he didn't have time to turn around and reassure her. He stood next to the door, watching for any movement outside, looking for any telltale hints that they weren't alone.

He scanned the room, looking for the safest place. Whoever had designed the cabin had scenic views in mind, not safety. There were way too many windows. "Willa, move over closer to the fireplace," he said in a low voice.

Without questioning him, she moved over and sat on the floor, leaning against the stone that soared to the ceiling. It was the best he could do. He wanted her in his sight.

He stood next to the door, waiting patiently as the lights flickered two more times. Each time, it took longer for them to come back on. If someone was out there, manipulating the generator, it was a good strategy, he acknowledged. Sooner or later, he would have to leave the cabin to check on the generator. And then the perpetrator would pounce.

The lights flickered one more time, then stayed out. The cabin plunged into darkness, the only light coming from the flickering fire. Griff tensed. If no one came out of the cabin now, the person waiting outside would be forced to make his move.

Nothing happened. There was no movement outside, no appearances of shadows darker than they should be. There were no sounds from outside, either. And Griff knew he would hear something if someone was outside the cabin. The kidnappers who were after Willa wouldn't know how to move noiselessly through the night. They weren't professionals. He was sure of it. He was a professional, and he knew what to look for. Willa's kidnappers had given up far too easily when they'd had her the first time.

He waited an agonizing half hour, but still there was nothing. Finally he whispered to Willa, "Come on over here. But stay low."

He heard her moving across the floor slowly; then she was at his side. He squeezed her shoulder, then let her go. He couldn't afford to be distracted. "Sit on the floor over against the cabinet." He nodded toward the tiny kitchen. He wanted her away from the outside wall. "I don't think there's anyone out there, but I'm not willing to take any chances."

"How would anyone have found us?" He could hear the tiny frisson of fear in her voice.

"There are about a thousand ways, if they're clever enough." He hadn't thought they were that clever, but he'd been wrong before. "I'm going to take a look outside."

"You're not going to leave me in here by myself, are you?" Even though she was whispering, he heard her voice rise.

"You can't come outside. You'll be a target."

"I'll be a sitting duck here in the house."

"I won't let anyone get into the house."

He imagined he could hear her swallow in the darkness. "All right. You're the expert, I guess. Tell me what to do."

"That's my girl." The words slipped out accidentally, but he told himself he meant nothing personal.

"I saw a torch in one of the drawers in the kitchen. See if you can find it."

"A torch?" she repeated.

"You Americans call it a 'flashlight,' I think."

He listened as she rummaged in first one drawer, then another. Finally he heard her murmur of satisfaction.

"Here it is."

"Good. I want you to sit in the corner of the kitchen, where there aren't any windows. If anyone but me comes in the house, there's a chance he won't see you at first. If he does, hold the torch as far away from your body as you can and shine it in his eyes. You'll blind him for a moment, and that will be your chance to get out the door."

The silence pulsed with her fear. Finally she said, "I can do that." There was a tremble in her voice, but her words were firm.

"I know you can, Willa." He wanted to crush her in his arms and tell her how brave she was, and how much he admired her. But he wouldn't allow himself to be distracted. So he deliberately looked away from her, examining the darkness outside the window once again. "It's not going to happen," he said. "But I want you to be prepared for anything."

"Go ahead and go," she said, and her voice was steadier. "I'm fine."

He couldn't stop himself from turning to look at her again. "I know you are, Willa. You're more than fine. You're incredible." He ached to touch her, but instead tightened his hand on the door. "I'll be back soon. Don't worry."

He slipped out the door before he could persuade himself to stay with Willa, to protect her. She wouldn't be safe until he made sure there was no one waiting for them outside the cabin.

He moved across the open yard in front of the cabin, feeling horribly exposed, then melted into the trees that surrounded the small building. There he waited.

The only sounds he heard were the sounds of night. Far in the distance, he heard the cry of a night predator. Above him, the needles of the pines rustled in the wind. The trees groaned as branches rubbed against trunks, the noise eerie in the darkness. But Griff ignored it, listening for any hint of an intruder in the night.

He waited for what seemed an eternity, but he heard no restless shifting of feet in the leaf litter on the ground. There was no smell of fear and excitement in the air, no taste of reckless bloodlust in the wind. They were alone at the cabin. No one had found their sanctuary in the mountains.

He circled the cabin, just to be sure, stopping every few feet to listen. But the results were always the same.

Finally he hurried back to the door of the cabin. Before he entered, he called out, "It's me, Willa. Griff. I'm coming back in."

As he stepped through the door of the cabin, Willa threw herself against him. "I was so worried," she said, her voice catching as she wrapped her arms around him and held on tightly. "I couldn't hear anything, and you were gone for so long. I was afraid that someone had ambushed you."

"I'm fine," he said, resting his face against her hair and stroking her back. "I'm sorry I scared you. I just wanted to be sure there wasn't anyone out there."

"I was terrified," she said as she curled her fingers into his shoulders. "I thought you might have been hurt, and I didn't know what to do."

"You did exactly what you were supposed to do," he said, gathering her close. "You stayed in here where I wouldn't have to worry about you."

He rubbed his cheek against the silk of her hair, inhaling her fragrance. She smelled like flowers and sunshine, and he couldn't get enough of her.

"Griff," she murmured, raising her head and tightening her arms around him.

Without thinking, without reasoning, he bent his head and met her mouth with his. He could think of nothing except his need to possess her, to assure himself she was all right. And she answered his kiss with a passion of her own. Her mouth opened beneath his, tasting him as eagerly as he savored her.

He felt her melt against him, her body subtly surrendering to his. Her breasts pressed against his chest, and his hands ached to feel their weight. Her hard nipples pressed into him, making him burn with need. When he trailed his fingers along her throat, her pulse galloped wildly against his hand. And when he bent to kiss her neck, she moaned his name.

Before he could think, before he could stop himself, he slid his hands beneath her sweater and along the warm satin of her skin. She inhaled sharply, and he felt her tense. But she clasped her arms around him and kissed him again.

He closed his eyes as his hands roamed over her back and sides. Her skin was hot and slick, and the pleasure coursing through him made his senses reel. He was lost in the feel of her, lost in the sensations she evoked.

He had to touch her or he would lose his mind. Her breasts were heavy in his hands, and her nipples were tight against the soft material of her bra. When he touched them lightly, she gasped against his mouth.

He fumbled with the front clasp, and when it fell open beneath his fingers, her satiny breasts tumbled into his hands. When he smoothed his thumbs over her nipples, they were hot.

"Griff!"

He drank in her cries of pleasure, hard and aching with the need to bury himself inside her. She was trembling in his arms, holding tightly to his shoulders, and when he opened his eyes to look at her, he saw that her face was filled with need.

Groaning, he bent his head to take her nipple in his mouth. She cried out again and pressed herself closer to him. He felt her hands pulling at his shirt, and finally her fingers were on his skin, touching and exploring.

He couldn't stop the shudder that ripped through him, could barely control the need to rip off her clothes and lay her down on the floor. He knew she wouldn't stop him. She was as aroused, as lost in him, as he was in her.

Closing his eyes, he swirled his tongue around her nipple again and surged against her. She clutched at his back and moaned his name again, and Griff pulled her close. But when she shivered once more, the haze of wanting faded from his brain just enough for her to realize that she was cold.

And that was enough to make him gentle his hold on her. He pulled her close for another instant, resting his head against her hair as he pulled her sweater back into place. He couldn't bear to let her go just yet.

"What's wrong?" she asked, and he could hear her need in the smoky huskiness of her voice, feel it in the flutter of her hands.

"Nothing. And everything."

She eased herself back far enough to look into his face, and he saw the uncertainty in her eyes. "What happened, Griff?"

"This is the wrong time and place for this," he managed to say. "I have to figure out what's wrong with the generator."

"I see." She tried to step away, but he held her tightly.

Suddenly he saw the doubt in her eyes, the vulnerability. And realized what she was thinking. "Don't think that I don't want you," he growled.

She swallowed, and he watched the ripple of her throat in the moonlight. "It's hard not to think that when you pull away every time we kiss."

"I want you so much I can barely stand," he said. He took her hand and pressed it against the rigid, throbbing ache in his jeans. "Does that feel like I don't want you?"

He'd expected her to flinch away, but instead she touched him lightly, her fingers exploring the length and hardness of him. He shuddered and closed his eyes as wave after wave of craving crashed over him. "Hell, Willa, stop. Or you're going to have me on my knees, begging."

Too slowly, she took her hand away. "You make me want to beg. I think I'd like to hear you beg, too." Her voice was shaking and filled with wonder.

He took a deep, ragged breath and moved away from her. His whole body ached and pulsed with need. "I can't do this, Willa. I can't allow myself to be distracted. A whole army of thugs could have come through this door, and I wouldn't have noticed." He reached out and touched her cheek, then pulled back. "And that's only for starters. You don't belong with a man like me."

"Says who?" She lifted her chin and glared at him defiantly.

"Says me." He turned away from the temptation of her swollen mouth and dark, pleading eyes. "You don't know who I am, Willa. Not really. And I don't ever want you to know."

"Maybe you don't know me, either." Her voice was husky. "Maybe we're more alike than either of us realize."

Seven

Griff crushed the spark of hope that flared up inside him. He would never be in the same class as Willa, never be worthy of her. "We need to go check on that generator."

Willa stared at him for a long time, then she nodded. "Let's do that."

She turned around to pick up the torch she'd left on the floor, and he stared at her, puzzled. He'd expected her to argue with him, to tell him he was exactly what she wanted—but she hadn't.

He felt a burst of disappointment. "Let's go, then," he said gruffly. "You'll have to hold the torch for me. This may take a while."

"That's all right. I'm very good at waiting," she said.

He gave her a sharp look, but she merely raised her eyebrows at him. Scowling, he stomped out the door and headed for the back of the cabin. Willa was right behind him.

The generator sat in a small enclosure at the rear of the building. He wanted to kick it. If it hadn't stopped running, he wouldn't have thought someone had found them. And if he hadn't been so worried about Willa, he never would have kissed her. He was horribly afraid that Willa had seen the truth, seen that he wanted her with an all-consuming need. He would have to be very careful not to touch her again.

"Hold the light here," he said, banishing his need from his mind, determined to concentrate only on the task at hand. He gestured at the machine in front of him. Willa squatted down next to him and held the beam of the torch on the generator.

Griff inventoried each part with his hands and his eyes. Nothing looked broken or out of place. He checked to make sure there was enough fuel; the tank was at least half full. Grunting, he lay down on the ground and peered around the edge of the enclosure that protected the generator from the weather.

And swore long and loud.

"What did you find?" Willa scooted closer and tried to peer over his shoulder.

"The damn belt is broken," he growled.

He reached behind the generator and pulled out the frayed and separated belt of rubber. "It must have gotten caught a couple of times before it broke completely, and that's why the lights flickered, then came back on."

"Well, at least it's something fixable," she said, standing up and switching off the torch.

"*If* there's another belt." He scowled again and held out his hand. "Let me have the torch. I'll check in the shed."

He stalked away, lighting the way with the thin beam of light. The torch barely illuminated the shed, but he was able to search through the drawers of the workbench, and he could see there was no spare belt anywhere.

"No belt," he told Willa, who waited by the door. "Let's go back in the house."

She followed him silently. Once inside, he carefully locked the door, then turned to her. "Let's go sit near the fire. You're probably getting cold."

"I'm fine," she said, but he saw her shiver as she headed for the fireplace. Willa was far tougher and stronger than he had ever imagined. He couldn't believe he'd thought of her as a soft, easily trampled flower. She was proving to be more like a proud, supple tree, bending with the wind, but never breaking.

They sat in front of the fireplace as he examined the broken belt. He'd worked enough with small engines to know how to fix them, and how to jerry-rig them to keep them running. There was no way it could be repaired.

"This one is completely shot," he said finally.

Willa leaned closer to look, and although he tried not to notice, her scent surrounded him. "What are our options?"

"We can go without electricity, or we can get a new belt." He scowled again. "I don't like either of those ideas."

"It's not that cold. We can survive without the heat."

Admiration stirred again, but he ruthlessly pushed it away. "It's not just the heat. It's the pump for the water, and the electricity for the stove, and lights. Not to mention that if we don't have electricity, we've lost our ability to communicate. I'm not sure this type of phone will work without electricity.''

''So we need another belt. Can we get one in El Paso?''

He nodded grimly. ''We can get a belt there. That's not what I'm worried about.''

''Then what?'' She rested her chin in her hand and stared at him.

''If we leave this cabin and go to El Paso, we're taking a chance. We're safe here, because no one but Ryan knows where we are. What if someone you know sees you in El Paso? And what if they tell someone else? I don't like it.'' He scowled again.

''I don't know that many people, Griff,'' she protested. ''The chances of running into someone I know are pretty slight.''

''How many students did you have in your classes last semester?'' he asked.

She shrugged. ''I had three classes, and there were between twenty and forty people in each of them.''

''That's a hundred people, right there.'' He stood up and paced around the small room. ''And if you start adding in friends and acquaintances, there's a lot more of them. Maybe none of them are in El Paso right now, but maybe some of them are. And maybe we'd only run into one of them. But that's one too many.''

''I'm sorry,'' she said softly. ''It must be horrible to have to think like that every day.''

He hadn't thought of it that way before. And he couldn't afford to think about it now. "That's just the way it is." He sat down abruptly. "We can't do anything about the belt tonight. I'm afraid it's going to be cold in here."

"I'll survive," she said lightly. "There are probably extra blankets somewhere."

He looked into the fire. "Do you want to sleep in the same bed? Just to keep warm? Two bodies are always warmer than one." His voice had an edge to it.

Silence stretched between them, and finally he glanced over at her. He couldn't read her expression. She met his gaze, and held it. He looked away first.

"I don't think so," she said, and her voice was husky. The flickering firelight reflected off her face, making her eyes appear huge and mysterious. "I don't think that would be a good idea, Griff."

"I can control myself."

"I know," she murmured. "You've demonstrated that more than once."

"Then what's the problem?"

"Do you really have to ask?"

No, he didn't. He wanted to sleep in the same bed with Willa almost more than he wanted to breathe. But looking at Willa in the firelight, he knew there wouldn't be much sleeping if he crawled between the sheets with her.

"Then you should sleep out here, in front of the fire." He stood abruptly. Thinking about sleeping with Willa wasn't a good idea. "I'll get more fire-wood."

"All right."

When he returned with the wood, she was still sitting next to the fire. The cabin was definitely getting colder. By morning, it would be like a refrigerator. "Go get ready for bed while I build up the fire," he said, trying not to think about Willa in the oversize T-shirt she wore to bed.

"Where are you going to sleep?" she asked.

"Upstairs."

"It'll be cold up there. Why don't you sleep down here, near the fire? There's plenty of room for both of us."

"I don't think that's a good idea."

Even in the dim light from the fire, he could see her blush. "You're right. I don't know what I was thinking."

She was thinking the same thing he was thinking. Turning away from her before he could do or say something really crazy, he threw a log onto the fire with vicious accuracy. Willa hurried away, and he heard the door to the bedroom close with a tiny *click*.

She emerged a few minutes later, her T-shirt tantalizingly draped over her slender frame, her shapely legs tempting him. He saw that she'd left her socks on, and the picture she made was at once innocent and sexy.

He jerked away from her and tried to concentrate on arranging the logs on the fire. In a few minutes the fire was blazing and heat poured out of the fire-place.

"You should be set now," he said, standing and moving away from her. "If it gets cold during the night, call me and I'll put more logs on the fire."

"I'm perfectly capable of putting a log on the fire by myself," she said, arranging a blanket on the floor and being careful not to look at him. "But thanks for the offer."

"You're welcome." He watched her for a moment, wanting nothing more than to curl up next to her on the floor and pull her close. Shoving his hands into the pockets of his jeans, he turned away. "I'll see you in the morning."

"Good night, Griff."

Her voice was soft, and he heard an unmistakable yearning in her tone. Before he could stop himself, he turned around to look at her. "Sleep well, Willa."

Her gaze caught and held his, and she couldn't disguise the flash of need. Then she looked away. "You, too."

Her silhouette was reflected in the firelight, making her face shadowed and mysterious. But he wouldn't forget the desire that her eyes had revealed.

He'd think about it all night.

He forced himself to walk up the stairs to the loft before he could touch her again. Because if he touched her tonight, he wouldn't be able to stop at a few kisses. If he touched her tonight, they'd go places from which there was no turning back. And that couldn't happen.

It was cold in his room, but he welcomed it. The cold would keep his mind off Willa, keep his mind off the heat they could generate together. As he slipped between the chilled sheets on his bed, he thought once more about her, sleeping in front of the fire. He allowed himself to linger on the image for a moment, and then he banished it from his mind. If there was one thing he was good at, it was focusing on the job that had to be done.

It had just never been this hard before.

The house was cold and still when he woke with a jerk. Several hours had passed, he knew, since he'd fallen asleep. But something had startled him, and he lay quietly in the bed, listening.

The sound came again, a soft cry of distress, and he knew instantly that it was Willa. Shoving the blankets aside, he scrambled out of bed and grabbed his gun before running down the stairs. Nothing was out of place in the cabin. The door and all the windows were closed, and Willa appeared to be asleep on the floor in front of the fireplace.

Then she cried out again, a sound that tore his heart out. She was having a nightmare.

He hurried over to her side and dropped to the floor next to her. Her auburn hair tumbled around her face, and she moved restlessly on the blanket she'd spread on the floor. "Willa," he whispered, touching her shoulder. "Wake up."

She didn't open her eyes or respond. Instead, she gave another sharp cry, and tears began to run down her cheeks. "Willa," he said, more loudly. "You're having a nightmare. Wake up."

She wore a cardigan over her T-shirt for warmth, and her restless movements made it gape open in front. The neck of the T-shirt was scooped low on her chest, and when she turned toward him, he saw a flash of pale flesh. His whole body tightened painfully, then he carefully pulled her cardigan together again.

"Wake up, Willa."

Her eyelids fluttered open and she looked at him, but her eyes were curiously blank. "Griff," she murmured, and held out her arms.

She was still asleep, he realized. Without thinking, he lay down next to her and pulled her close to him. Wasn't it dangerous to wake a person having a nightmare? But only a monster would let her suffer through a nightmare alone, he told himself. She clearly wasn't going to wake up, so the next best thing was to comfort her while she slept.

She settled against him with a murmur of pleasure. Nestling her face into his neck, she pressed her hand against his chest and immediately fell into a sound sleep.

Her breathing changed as he held her. He felt it deepen and smooth from ragged to even and slow. She didn't cry out, didn't move. Apparently he'd chased the nightmare away. But now she was curled around him as if they belonged together, and the rest of the night was going to be *his* nightmare.

Or his dream come true.

How else could he describe the opportunity to hold Willa close, to savor the scent and feel of her? He closed his eyes and tried to ignore the insistent throbbing from certain areas of his body. Willa was asleep and safe. In the morning, she wouldn't even remember that he'd been holding her. He'd slip away before she woke up. So Griff allowed himself to hold her close, allowed himself to indulge his fantasies.

It was only one night, after all.

Willa woke up slowly, floating on a sea of pleasurable sensations. She was dreaming about Griff. His scent surrounded her, and his heart beat strong and steady against her cheek. She didn't want to open her eyes, afraid that the fantasy would burst like a bubble in the air.

Then her pillow moved, and she opened her eyes with a start. She was sprawled on top of Griff, her arms around his neck and her legs intimately tangled with his. Her head was pillowed against his chest, and the thin T-shirt he wore was no barrier against the heat that poured from his body.

In that first instant of realization, all she wanted to do was savor his closeness. She wanted to snuggle closer to him, to allow herself to sink into him. She didn't want to think about why he was sleeping next to her. She only wanted to enjoy it.

But Griff had seemed so determined to avoid getting involved with her. What had happened the night before? Something had, or he wouldn't have ended up next to her. But she suspected he wouldn't be happy about this, either.

So she shifted her legs slowly, trying to ease away from him before he woke up. She didn't want to make him uncomfortable—and the attraction that simmered between them definitely made him uncomfortable.

As she eased her leg from between his legs, she brushed against him and froze. Part of him was definitely awake. Slowly she looked up and found him watching her.

"Good morning," he said, his voice raspy with sleep.

"Good morning to you, too." She tried to make her voice light and careless, and was afraid she'd failed miserably.

"You had a nightmare last night," he said, his hands tightening on her as she tried to pull away. "I couldn't wake you up, so I decided to stay with you until you fell back to sleep. I guess I fell asleep, too."

"Thanks." She gave him a casual smile, and tried to pull away again.

"Anytime." His voice deepened, and his arms shifted around her, pulling her more snugly against him. "Do you remember what it was about?"

She shook her head. "No," she whispered. His hand was drifting slowly down her back, then brushing over her hip, and she was having a hard time speaking. "I don't remember."

"Do you have nightmares often?"

"I don't think so."

"It must be the kidnapping attempt."

"Hmm?" He'd burrowed his other hand beneath her cardigan and splayed his fingers against her side. Heat pulsed into her, spreading like liquid fire.

"I didn't mean to stay here for the rest of the night."

"It's all right," she managed to say. "I appreciate it."

"Do you?"

He nuzzled against her neck, and the stubble from his beard rasped against her skin. She shivered once, helplessly, as desire burst into life inside her.

"I know you were just being kind," she gasped.

"Kind?" His mouth drifted down her throat and his tongue dipped into the hollow above her collarbone. "I'm not kind, Willa."

"You've been very kind to me."

He raised his head and looked at her. "Is that what you think? That I'm kind to you?"

She nodded, unable to look away from the heat in his eyes. "Yes," she whispered.

"Kindness isn't what I feel for you," he muttered, then bent his head to her again. His mouth swept over her chest, exposed by the neck of her T-shirt. Suddenly he cupped her breast in one hand, his heat searing her through the thin material. Then he shoved the neck of her shirt down and took one of her nipples in his mouth.

She arched up to meet him, her primal need shocking her with its intensity. Griff shifted abruptly, pinning her beneath his weight. She felt the hard length of him probing against her, and she moved to accommodate him.

His hand trembled against her, then she felt him gather himself and withdraw from her. He pulled her T-shirt back up over her breast and smoothed his hand down her chest. "Time to get up," he said.

She scooted away from him and sat up, leaning against the couch as she watched him stand and look around. "What an interesting way to wake up in the morning."

He scowled at her. "It wasn't what I planned when I lay down with you, believe me."

"And here I was hoping," she murmured.

He gave her a sharp glance. "We've already discussed this, Willa. You know how I feel."

"No, Griff, I don't. If you want nothing to do with me, why did you stay with me last night? Why didn't you just wake me up, and go back to sleep? And why did you kiss me just now?"

"I already told you, I didn't mean to fall asleep with you last night. And I wasn't awake yet when I kissed you," he snapped. "I wasn't thinking."

"I like it when you don't think."

"It's dangerous when I don't think. I already told you why I can't get involved with you."

"And I told you that you were wrong. We're all alone here, Griff. No one knows where we are. You're not endangering me."

"That remains to be seen." He walked away and looked out the window. "Let's get going. I want to get into El Paso for that belt, and back as quickly as we can. The longer we're there, the more chance we have of being spotted.''

''All right.'' She scrambled to her feet. ''I'll change my clothes and we can go.'' She looked longingly at the kitchen. ''I suppose there's no time to make coffee, is there?''

He turned around, and his face softened. ''We'll stop at a take-away restaurant and get some.''

''What's a take-away restaurant?''

''Someplace that has a window where you stay in your car and order your food. They're all over in America.''

''A drive-thru.'' Her lips twitched. ''I'll hold you to that.''

She turned and hurried into her bedroom. She saw her breath in the air, and realized Griff was right. It got too cold at night in the mountains to stay here without a working generator.

In ten minutes she was ready to go, and she emerged into the living room in time to see Griff strapping himself into a shoulder holster. He slid his gun into it, then put on his jacket.

''Are you sure you can carry that gun around here?'' she asked, fascinated in spite of herself. He seemed so comfortable carrying the ugly, deadly weapon.

''Believe me, Willa, if I have to use it, the kidnappers aren't going to ask me if I have a permit.''

''What if the police see it?''

''They won't see it unless I want them to see it.

And that's not going to happen.'' He grabbed the broken belt and shoved it into his pocket. "Let's go."

They drove in silence down the trail that led to the road. Griff had distanced himself from her after he'd kissed her that morning, but she was very aware of him in the close confines of his truck. If she reached out a hand, she would touch his thigh. When he shifted gears, his hand almost touched her.

By the time they reached the outskirts of El Paso, the truck felt much too warm. She was relieved when they saw the first buildings. She needed a distraction from Griff's presence.

"There's a place we can get coffee," she said.

He glanced at it and kept on going. "Not there."

"What was wrong with that place?"

"There aren't any people in line. We want to go to a place where there's a lot of business. Where they serve one person after another. That way they'll be less likely to remember one person or any particular car."

"You'd better let me drive, then, and order. Anyone will notice your accent."

He gave her a sharp glance, but nodded reluctantly. "You're right." He looked out the window and pulled into a parking lot. "Here's a place with a lot of business."

He stopped in the parking lot beneath the familiar red-and-yellow sign, and they quickly switched places. Then Willa drove into line at the drive-thru.

"Do you want anything besides coffee?" she asked.

He gestured at the menu. "A couple of those breakfast sandwich things."

When they got close to the window, he said quietly, "Don't let the person at the window get a good look at you. Give him the money, take your food and coffee, and look away as quickly as possible. And if there's a problem with your order, for God's sake, don't say anything."

Her hands clenched the steering wheel as they crept closer to the order window. She had her money ready, and the young man who took it gave her the change quickly, looking bored. When he handed her the sacks of food and cups of coffee, she thanked him and turned to hand the bags to Griff.

Without looking back at the young man, she drove away and parked in the lot once more. Then she and Griff switched places again. Sitting back on the passenger side of the truck, she leaned against the seat, her heart pounding. When she took the cup of coffee that Griff handed her, some of the dark liquid slopped over the side of the cup. Her hands were shaking, she realized.

"I guess I'm not cut out for this spy stuff," she said weakly.

"You did great." His voice was soft and intimate in the small cab of the truck. "You did exactly what you needed to do."

"You mean I have a future as a secret agent?"

He studied her for a moment, then, to her surprise, smiled.

"I hope not. You'd terrorize everyone in the business. They wouldn't know what to make of you."

"I hope that's a compliment," she said, trying to make her voice light.

"Absolutely, Blue." He handed her the sack containing her pastry. "Let's eat. I know you're already suffering from coffee deprivation."

Fifteen minutes later they were back on the road, looking for a home-improvement store. "I've seen those huge stores," Griff said. "They'll probably have what we need, and they're so busy that no one will remember us." He changed lanes and turned into a parking lot. "Here's one."

They found a display of black rubber belts of various sizes, and spent about ten minutes searching for one that appeared to be the same size as the broken belt from the generator. "Now we need to find one a little bigger, and one a little smaller," Griff said.

"Whatever for?"

"Just in case this one doesn't work. We don't want to have to come back here."

"Good thinking," she said.

He grunted as he sorted through the sizes of belts. It didn't take long to find several in slightly different sizes. "These'll do. Let's take all of them."

"All right."

As they walked through the store, they saw a clerk with a stack of boxes ahead of them, staggering up the aisle. They both moved to the side, pressing against the display rack so that he could pass, but he tripped on something and the boxes tumbled from his arms.

"Oh, God, I'm sorry." The young man turned to them, his face bright red. "Did I hurt you?"

"We're fine," Willa said with a smile. "None of them touched us."

The clerk's eyes widened as he looked more closely at her. Then his mouth fell open. "Dr. Simms?" he said.

Eight

Willa felt herself pale as she recognized one of her students from the previous semester. "Pete." Her voice was faint. "What are you doing here?"

"Making some money over Christmas break," he answered cheerfully. He seemed to have gotten over his embarrassment at dropping the boxes. "How about you?"

"We're, ah, on our way to California for the holidays, and we realized we needed a few things," she improvised desperately. "We figured we could find it here."

"We've got just about everything," the young man said, his voice proud. "Can I help you find the part you need?"

"No, we're all set," she said quickly.

"Then have a good trip," he said, bending to pick up the boxes. "Maybe I'll be taking one of your classes next semester."

"That would be nice," she said, as Griff pulled her away. They hurried around a corner before Pete could say anything more.

"Hell." Griff proceeded to let out a long string of curses. "What damn bad luck."

"I thought you were being ridiculous to worry about seeing someone I knew," she said in a low voice. "I can't believe we ran into Pete."

"You did a good job," he said gruffly. "Telling him we were on our way to California was a stroke of genius."

"It was the only thing I could think of," she admitted.

They had reached the checkout counter, and Griff didn't say anything while he paid for the belts.

When they were back in the parking lot, he took her hand and twined their fingers. "It's probably all right," he said softly. "Pete will remember seeing you, but the chances of anyone asking him about it are very small. And if anyone does ask, he'll tell them we're on our way to California."

"So there isn't going to be a small army of heavily armed men storming the cabin in a few hours?"

His lips twitched. "I had no idea you had such a melodramatic mind. No, I think we're probably still safe. But we'll have to be careful for the next few days. And it was a good lesson in why we need to stay away from El Paso. It was just bad luck that we ran into Pete. We don't want to take any more chances like that."

"We should probably stock up on groceries while we're here, then."

Griff opened the door to his truck, then swung into the driver's seat. He drummed his fingers on the steering wheel as he thought, then finally turned to her. "You're right. If we wait until the afternoon when it's busier, there'll be less chance of someone remembering us. But there's more chance to run into someone you know. So let's go find a grocery store.''

They hurried through a large grocery store, tossing whatever they thought they would need into the cart. The bored check-out clerk snapped her gum and barely looked at them while she scanned their groceries, and they were back in the truck in less than a half hour.

"Let's get out of here," Griff said, and they headed for the edge of town.

Willa watched him as he drove, and noticed he constantly checked the rearview mirror. Neither of them spoke, and tension wound tighter and tighter in the truck. Finally, when he glanced in the rearview mirror one more time, Willa said, "Is someone behind us?"

"There are a couple of trucks." He spoke through his teeth. "We haven't gotten far enough off the main road yet to really worry, but I don't like the way these two are sticking to our tail."

"So what do we do?"

"We keep driving, and watch them."

Several miles before the turnoff for the cabin, Griff slowed the truck, then pulled over to the side of the road. "I need to get a look at these two," he muttered. Keeping one eye on the rearview mirror, he reached for Willa. "It's show time, sweetheart."

Before she had a chance to ask him what he meant, he pulled her into his arms and fastened his mouth to hers. Her heart began to pound, and she reached up and twined her arms around his neck. But there was no passion in his kiss, no feeling. In fact, he was staring out the side window of the truck as his mouth moved on hers.

"What's going on?" she managed to say.

"It's all for show," he muttered, lifting his mouth away from hers only far enough to speak. "I want to see who's behind us, and I want them to think we're not paying attention."

"Oh."

Deflated, she felt like an utter fool. But she held onto him, knowing she had to play the part. As the rumble of the first truck became louder, she felt him tense in her arms. He lifted his mouth away from hers, and she felt him staring over her shoulder.

Then the sound of the second truck approached, and he kissed her again. But his eyes were wide open, and she wasn't certain he even realized he was touching her. She was his cover, his prop, and his hands were completely impersonal.

The second truck rolled past, and as its sound faded into the distance, she could feel Griff relaxing. Finally he flexed his hands on her shoulders, and leaned back to look at her.

"They're gone."

"I heard." Resolutely pushing her need for him into the background, she tried to give him a smile. "Did you see anything?"

"Just a couple of Texas boys driving their pickup trucks. They weren't interested in us at all."

"So we're safe for now?"

"That remains to be seen." His eyes darkened, and

he slowly drew her closer again. "I'm sorry I had to do that, Willa."

"You weren't even thinking about kissing me," she burst out, then felt her face redden. "I mean, I knew it was just for show. I knew you were just using me as a prop. It's all right, Griff. There's nothing to apologize for."

"I think there is." He bent his head slowly, staring into her eyes. Her heart raced and her pulse thundered in her ears. "When I kiss you, Willa, I don't *want* to think about anything, or anyone, but you. I want to take the time to enjoy you. I want you to know I'm kissing you."

He didn't have to worry about that, she thought as her heart gave a little hiccup. Her pulse skittered when he merely looked at her. When he touched her, her heart rate went off the charts.

"Believe me, Griff, I know when you're kissing me." She tried to sound cool, but she was afraid her words came out wobbly and unsteady.

"Are you sure?"

His whisper was seductive, and as he bent his head to her mouth, she felt herself falling helplessly into him. Yes, she was sure. No one but Griff had ever evoked this instant response, this immediate blaze of desire. And she was afraid no one else ever would.

He crushed her mouth beneath him, his hands claiming her as his. A hot spike of arousal leapt to life inside her and she pressed closer to him. He groaned into her mouth, kissing her once more, then slowly eased away.

"We have to get back to the cabin before someone else comes along." His voice was thick with ardour, and his eyes burned. "We can't stay here."

"I know."

He let her go, but she felt his reluctance in the lingering caress of his hands. Then suddenly he turned and restarted the truck, pulling out onto the road with a squeal of tires and a grinding of gears.

He tore up the road, barely slowing his speed when they got to the track that led to the cabin. Willa held onto the strap above the door as they bounced over the holes and rocks in the road.

When they were almost at the cabin, Griff slowed the truck and looked over at her. "Sorry, Willa," he said. "I was taking out my aggression. I didn't mean to give you such a rough ride."

"That's all right," she managed to say. "I won't break."

"No, you won't, will you," he murmured.

She looked over at him sharply, but he was staring straight ahead, out the windshield. There had been longing and regret in his voice, and she wondered why.

When they reached the cabin, he stopped the car in front, and jumped out. "Wait here," he told her. "I'm going to check on things."

He circled the cabin, peering at every window, then disappeared into the trees surrounding their small clearing. Finally he returned to the truck and climbed back in. "No one's been around since we've been gone," he said as he drove the truck into the shed.

"Great. Let's get that generator going." If he could ignore what had happened on the road, she could, too, she thought.

It only took a few minutes to replace the belt and get the generator started again. But instead of heading back into the cabin, Griff said, "I'm going to chop some more firewood. We used up a lot last night."

There was still a huge pile of logs stacked against the side of the cabin, but she didn't say anything. She only nodded. "Good idea. I'll help."

He narrowed his eyes. "There's only one splitter and ax," he said. "Why don't you wait in the cabin?"

"Because it's cold in there. I'd rather be out here, working."

He scowled at her. "Well, I don't need any help."

"I'll stack the wood after you chop it," she said, ignoring his words. "I'm going to see if there are any gloves in the shed."

A few minutes later she walked out of the shed, pulling on a pair of worn leather work gloves. Griff was already chopping wood. He'd stripped down to his T-shirt, and the black material already clung to him, wet with sweat down his back.

His muscles rippled in the sunlight, and his brown hair gleamed with golden highlights. She stood and watched him for a moment, feeling her own yearnings stir. But it wasn't just the external package that attracted her to Griff. She'd met plenty of other men who were good-looking and had great bodies. It was the person inside who interested her, the complicated man full of both strength and vulnerability.

And he was interested in her. He wanted to deny it, but she could taste it in his kisses, feel it in the way he touched her, the way he held her. Her heart raced as she walked toward him, but she managed to give him an easy smile.

"Kick the wood out to me when you split it, and I'll stack it."

He grunted at her, but he shoved the wood toward her with his foot. She picked it up and stacked it in the already huge pile next to the house. She didn't mind working outside. The air was cool, but the sun, shining in a cloudless sky, warmed her as she worked.

It wasn't long before she took off her jacket, and as she worked she felt herself beginning to sweat. Rolling up the sleeves of her shirt, she grabbed another log and slung it onto the pile.

Abruptly Griff said, "That's enough, I guess."

She straightened and looked over at him. His face was flushed, but it wasn't with exertion. His eyes glittered and his jaw worked as he looked at her.

"It's time to go into the house."

"What's wrong?" she asked.

He stared at her for a moment, then he turned and dropped the ax. "I can't watch you for another moment," he said, his voice rough. "I wanted to chop wood to get my mind off you, but I can't think of anything but you. I'm getting careless, and it's time to go into the house."

"All right." She slipped off the work gloves, staring at his back. "I'll put the tools away."

"No, I'll do it. Give me your gloves."

He tore them out of her hand, then picked up the ax and splitter and loped off to the shed. She waited for what seemed like a long time, but he didn't come back out, so she finally walked into the cabin.

She had sandwiches made when he finally returned. After washing his hands, he looked at the plates of sandwiches, his expression softening. "Thank you for making lunch, Willa."

"You're welcome. But don't act as if it's such a big deal. You're going to clean up."

His lips curved. "Fair enough."

They ate in silence, but the memory of his words outside lingered between them. Willa swallowed another bite of her sandwich, desperately searching her mind for something innocuous to say.

"It's getting warm in here, isn't it?" As soon as the words were out of her mouth, she flushed. "I mean, the generator is working just fine."

"I was hot before I came inside."

Willa squirmed in her chair. "Hard work will do that."

"Among other things."

The message in his eyes was unmistakable, and she stared at him, unable to look away.

Then he pushed away from the table. "I'll clean up in here, then I have some things to do outside."

"All right," she said faintly.

The cabin was suddenly far too small. Tension radiated from Griff as he stood at the sink and washed the dishes. She wanted to touch him, to ask him what he was thinking, but she couldn't move from her chair.

Did she really want to know the answer? Griff was attracted to her. What if he told her that he wanted to make love with her, but he wasn't interested in any kind of long-term relationship? What would she do?

She was terribly afraid she *knew* what she would do, and her heart ached at the thought. She was afraid that she would take whatever Griff offered, on whatever terms he offered it.

What had made her so needy, so willing to settle for crumbs? What had made her so willing to compromise her beliefs? Never before had she been interested in sex without commitment. She didn't want to think about that, either.

So she stood and moved to the window. She couldn't bear to sit so close to him, to feel the sexual energy that emanated from him. She couldn't bear to look at him right now, because all she would see were the flaws in her own character that would permit her to want a man who wasn't interested in the long term.

"I'll be back in a while," he said, and she didn't turn around. "Stay in the cabin."

"It's not like there are a lot of places to go up here." Her voice was more curt than she meant it to be, but maybe that was for the best.

"I'll be close by."

The door closed softly behind him. As she looked out the window, she saw him disappear into the trees.

A few minutes later she saw him on the mountain behind the house. She watched as he climbed steadily upward, then she deliberately turned away and picked up a book from the bookcase. She sat down, determined to read. But she stared at the same page for a long time.

Griff hiked steadily upward, refusing to slow down, refusing to stop even when his breathing became ragged and sweat poured down his back. He stripped off his shirt, tied it around his waist and kept on walking.

Finally he was high enough to look down and see the cabin, a miniature house set among toy trees, and he allowed himself to stop. He was far enough away now, out of reach of the temptation that was Willa.

He was far enough away that he could think this through without her distracting presence.

What the hell was the matter with him? He sank down onto a sun-warmed stone, but couldn't take his eyes off the cabin below. He'd made the mistake of falling asleep with her last night, and ever since he'd woken up tangled together with her this morning, all he could think about was laying Willa down on the closest horizontal surface and picking up where they'd left off.

He knew Willa was out of his reach. He knew it would be a huge mistake to get involved with her. It would end with nothing but heartbreak for Willa, and it would distract him from the job he needed to do. He couldn't be the kind of man she needed, the kind of man she deserved.

But that didn't seem to matter anymore. All his caution seemed to have flown out the window. It had taken just one look this morning at her beautiful, vulnerable face, nestled close to him with complete trust, and he'd been lost.

And worst of all, now she knew that he wanted her. Before today, he could pretend that she didn't matter. He could pretend that he didn't want her, that the wanting was all on Willa's side. But now he didn't even have that shield. He knew damn well that she'd seen the desire in his eyes, felt it in his touch.

So how were they supposed to get through the days—and nights—until Ryan found her would-be kidnappers? How was he supposed to not touch her?

He kicked a rock and listened with brooding satisfaction as it tumbled down the hill. He'd have to stay away from her.

But how could he do that if he was supposed to be protecting her?

He'd have to invent a lot of outside chores. And keep *her* in the house.

And that was going to be tougher than he'd originally thought. Willa had a mind of her own. She didn't hesitate to tell him when she thought he was wrong. And she wasn't the kind of woman who would stay obediently in the house when he told her to do so.

The need he felt for her terrified him. He'd faced down death in a dark, stinking alley with less fear. But somehow, in the last few days, Willa had managed to sneak into his soul, to touch him in a place no other woman had ever gone.

And he was afraid there was no turning back. Willa would always linger inside him, a memory that would creep up on him in the middle of the night, when he least expected it.

If he were smart, it would go no farther than this. If he were smart, Willa would never know how she'd managed to touch him. They would spend whatever time they had left at the cabin avoiding each other, and when Willa went back to College Station, he'd run as far and as fast as he could. He'd run all the way back to Australia, if he had to.

Yet he was terribly afraid that he wasn't smart at all. He was afraid that the next time Willa touched him, or the next time he touched her, he wouldn't be able to let go. He was afraid that he'd take a step that he'd regret forever.

And so would Willa.

They had no future. There was no forever for him and Willa.

He forced himself to stand and start walking back down the mountain. He couldn't stay up here for days or weeks until it was safe to go back to College Station. He'd have to face Willa sometime. It might as well be now.

Everyone said he had more willpower than any man they'd ever met. It was time to test that willpower.

Darkness was settling over the mountain when Griffin dried the last of the dinner dishes and slid them back into the cabinet. Willa had curled up on the couch and had picked up her book again. She'd been reading it all afternoon, but he didn't think she'd turned many pages. They had avoided each other since he'd walked back into the cabin, but the atmosphere was still unsettled and restless.

"Do you want me to start a fire?" he asked.

She looked up from her book, her eyes wary. He didn't blame her. He'd hardly spoken two words to her all afternoon. "If you'd like to."

"Might as well," he muttered. "We have plenty of wood."

"If we use it up, you can always chop more," she said sweetly. "We make a good team when it comes to chopping wood."

He stormed out the door, and returned a minute later with his arms full of logs. "Did anyone ever tell you that you have a smart mouth?"

"As a matter of fact, no. I guess you bring out the best in me."

He tossed three more logs on the fire, then squatted in front of the fireplace for a while, pushing at them with the poker. Finally he stood and paced to the window. It was almost completely dark. The trees pressed in on the house, and he could barely see the mountain behind them.

"I'm going to take a look around the house," he said abruptly.

She looked up, apprehension in her eyes. "Is something wrong?"

"No." He grabbed his coat and headed for the door. "I want to make sure it stays that way."

Nothing had disturbed the area around the cabin. It didn't take him long to realize that. But he kept moving through the trees, memorizing landmarks, telling himself that it was smart to know the area. Their lives might depend on it.

But he couldn't put off going back into the cabin forever. Finally he slipped back inside, hoping that Willa had gone to bed. But she was still sitting in front of the fireplace, staring at the pages of her book.

"Have you actually read any of that book today?" he asked.

She looked up at him, startled. "Of course I have."

"I would have thought a college professor would read a lot faster than that."

A slow flush crept up her neck and onto her face. "I've been distracted today." She sat up straighter and looked him in the eye. "Kind of like you, I guess."

"I haven't been distracted." As soon as the words were out of his mouth, he knew he'd made a mistake. He tried to cover himself. "It's my job to make sure the house is safe."

"Spare me, Griff." She didn't take her eyes off him. "You were making sure the cabin was safe from the top of the mountain?"

He threw himself into the chair across the room from the couch. He didn't intend to get any closer to Willa than this. "All right, I was restless. I'll admit it. I'm not used to sitting and doing nothing."

Her face softened as she watched him. "I'm not, either." She actually smiled. "We're quite a pair, aren't we?"

"A couple of work addicts," he said sourly. He was happy she'd made the assumption that he missed working. It took her attention away from the real issue. "I should have let you bring some work with you. Then you wouldn't be so bored."

"I never said I was bored," she said gently. "And I'm glad I didn't bring any work. That part of my life seems so far away."

"Tell me about being a college professor," he said, settling back in the chair and watching her face. "Is it what you've always wanted to do?" If they could talk about a different subject, maybe he could wrestle his mind away from the way she looked, her face flushed by the firelight and her glasses slipping down her nose. Maybe she could distract him from what he really wanted to do.

"My job?" She stared into the fire, a faraway look on her face. "You don't want to hear about that. It's a pretty boring subject."

"If you feel that way, why do you do it?" He watched her with genuine curiosity.

She didn't say anything for a long time, then she sighed. "For my father, I guess. He was desperate to see me settled in one place, with a stable job. It was his reaction to the life we had led."

"How do you mean?"

She roused herself and smiled at him. "My mother left us shortly after I was born. So it was just my father and me while I was growing up. He was in the army, and they sent him all over the world. I was a typical army brat. I never went to one school more than two years in a row. Just as soon as I got used to one place, we had to move again.''

"You must have hated that.''

She shook her head, her mouth still curved into a faint smile as she stared into the fire again. "Strangely enough, I didn't. Part of it was because I never knew any other kind of life, of course, but part of me loved the excitement or adventure of it—the fresh beginning every couple of years. I was far more adventurous than my father ever realized.

"He always felt guilty for dragging me around the world with him. Then he got sick right after I graduated from college. Soon after I got my master's degree and started my PhD program, he passed away. By that time, I had already invested a lot of time and effort in getting my degree. Toward the end of his illness, he became obsessed with the idea of my becoming a college professor. It was his idea of the perfect life—teach and stay in one place for the rest of your life. It was the most stable job he could imagine.''

"And stability is important to you.'' Griff held his breath, waiting for her answer.

Nine

"It was important to my father," she said. "I haven't figured out yet how important it is to me. But I did accept a tenure-track position at the university." She stared into the fire. "My father was so proud of me when I entered the master's program in political science. He would be ready to burst with pride if he were still alive."

"It sounds as if your life is a dream come true." Griff turned away and poked at the fire again, hiding his reaction from Willa. Disillusionment was a bitter taste on his tongue. What had he expected? he asked himself savagely. It was a long, hard road to become a college professor. And Willa had not only her own career aspirations, but also the hopes of her father riding on her slender shoulders.

She might not have intended her message to be quite so blunt, but nothing could have demonstrated their unsuitability for each other more clearly. She was a woman with a career, one she'd worked long and hard to attain. He was a man whose job took him around the world, often for months at a time. He lived with constant danger and spent his time with the dregs of society—people who Willa wouldn't even know existed. Willa would be horrified if she knew about his colleagues, knew what kind of people they were.

He needed to hear this, he told himself as he gave one of the logs a vicious shove. He needed this reminder of just how different he and Willa were.

Then he realized she hadn't responded to his statement. He swiveled around to face her. She stared into the fire, her face troubled.

"What's wrong?" he asked.

She gave him a faint smile. "You said my life is a dream come true, and I guess it is. I'm just not sure whose dream it is."

"I thought you loved your job."

"I suppose I do. I love teaching. I love being there that moment when a student suddenly 'gets it.' I love knowing that I'm helping someone learn." She shoved her hair away from her face and gave a shaky laugh. "I'm just being silly. We don't have enough to do here in this cabin. It's given me way too much time to think. That's always dangerous," she said lightly.

He wanted to stand and go to her, to sit next to her and wrap his arms around her. He wanted to have the right to comfort her, the right to listen to her dreams and share his with her.

But he was a man without any dreams, he reminded himself harshly. He had seen too much ugliness in his life to have any dreams left. He was a man who lived in a world of shadows and darkness, a world he couldn't ask any woman to embrace. And especially not a woman like Willa.

So he stared at the flames leaping in the fireplace and tightened his grip on the poker. "Your father was right to be proud of you," he said, but he didn't turn around to look at her. "You're a remarkable woman, Willa."

"Now you sound like one of my students when they're angling for a higher grade." Her voice was teasing, and he slowly turned to look at her. "I guess you have too much time on your hands, too."

He had far too much time on his hands, especially since he'd been able to think about only one thing lately—Willa. But he'd just been given another lesson in why Willa was exactly the wrong woman for him. So he stood and strolled to the window. It was the farthest place in the room from Willa.

"I'm sorry you're in this position," he said, and genuine regret filled his voice. He wished he weren't here with Willa. He wished he'd never gotten to know her like this. When she had been a college professor who appeared only occasionally at the Fortune ranch, he could fantasize about her, but he didn't have this gut-deep, aching need for her. If he'd never gotten to know Willa, he wouldn't have to deal with the gaping hole her absence would make in his life.

"Hey, don't worry about it," she said. "I'm thankful that you came along when you did. I don't want to think about what might have happened if you hadn't come to College Station that night."

He didn't want to think about it, either. "I'll call Ryan tomorrow or the next day. Maybe he's found something out that will help us figure out who those people were.'' He knew, though, that if Ryan had learned anything, he would have called.

"It's all right," she said gently. "Ryan will call when he has something to tell us. In the meantime, we'll survive in this cabin."

Speak for yourself. He turned away to look out the window. He wasn't sure how much more of this torture he could take.

"Tell me about yourself," she said from the couch.

He turned around to look at her. "What do you want to know?"

She shrugged. "Tell me what's important to Griffin Fortune."

He hesitated for a moment, then he crossed over to sit on the chair across from her. He'd tell her what was important to him. In fact, that was a wonderful idea—in case she still had any ideas about having some kind of relationship with him, he'd tell her exactly who he was. If that didn't make her run far and fast, he didn't know what would.

"I'm not really a Fortune," he began.

She cocked her head. "What do you mean?"

"Teddy and Fiona Fortune adopted me when I was about seven years old. Actually, I'm not sure they ever even went through the legal formalities. They took me in and raised me."

"I know that. But what do you mean that you're not really a Fortune?"

He scowled and looked away. "I mean, I'm not related to the Fortunes by blood."

Willa smiled at him. "Don't you know that blood

ties are the least important? What matters are the people who raise you and the values they give you. What matters is the man or the woman who tucks you into bed at night and listens to you when you need to talk. What matters are the people who were there for you when you were growing up. And the Fortunes were those people. You're just as much a Fortune as your sister Matilda and your brothers Brody and Reed."

"You don't know what I come from. Hell, neither do I."

"Where or what you come from doesn't matter nearly as much as where you end up. And I'd say you ended up in a pretty good place."

"Has anyone ever told you how Teddy found me?" He had to make her see.

"No, all I heard was that you were adopted."

"Willa, I don't even know my real name. I have no memory of my life before Teddy found me. And that's literally what happened. He found me sleeping under a bush on a remote part of his ranch. I was filthy dirty and wearing nothing but rags. I didn't even have any shoes, and it was early spring." He paused, waiting for the memories to come, but they never did. It was as if the entire first seven years of his life had been erased, leaving nothing behind. His first memory was waking beneath that bush and seeing Teddy Fortune crouching next to him.

"You're lucky that Teddy found you," she said softly.

"I'm damn lucky. I had been beaten, badly. I had

a broken collarbone, a broken arm, and I was covered with bruises. Teddy took me back to his wife Fiona.''

"And she took you in.''

"It didn't matter that she already had four sons. Christopher was only a baby at the time, but she took care of me like I was one of her own children. Teddy tried to find out who I was and where I belonged, but there was no trace of me. He always says it was like I just appeared out of the blue, a gift to the Fortunes.''

"I think I'd like your parents," she said softly.

"They're wonderful," he said gruffly. "I didn't speak when I first went to them. No one knew why, and not even the doctors could give them an answer. But it didn't matter to Teddy and Fiona. They made me feel like I belonged with them.''

"And you did." Willa's face glowed, and he looked away.

"I was a troublemaker," he said harshly. "Reed and Brody were afraid of me. Max didn't trust me. The baby didn't know enough to be scared, but he should have been. I'm sure I gave my parents plenty of sleepless nights.''

"What changed things with your family?" she asked.

He looked away. "I started school in the fall. They didn't know what grade to put me in, because I couldn't talk, but they put me in a class based on my size. No one bothered me. I think all the other kids were afraid of me, too. I didn't know my real name, so my parents named me Griffin because I was so wild. Then one day an older boy tried to pick on

Brody. This boy was a bully, but he'd left me alone. I guess he thought Brody would be an easier target because he was younger.''

She leaned forward. ''What happened?''

''I heard the commotion and went over to see what was going on. Brody was trying to defend himself, but the other boy was at least three years older than Brody, and a lot bigger. Some of his friends were holding Reed to keep him from helping Brody.''

His eyes darkened. He still remembered the anger that had boiled over when he saw the younger Brody being pushed around. ''I beat the boy bloody. It took three other boys to pull me off him. I stood there glaring at all of them, then asked if anyone else wanted to pick on a Fortune. I was shocked when the sounds of the words came out of my mouth. For a moment, no one moved. Then Reed came over and stood next to me, then Brody.''

He shrugged, trying to lighten the atmosphere. He hadn't meant to tell her so graphically what had happened. ''Ever since, the three of us have been close.''

''I heard you were inseparable.''

He shrugged again, uncomfortable with the admiration in her face. ''We stuck together. We lived a long way from town. Even in this country, I suspect farm and ranch kids are close to their brothers and sisters. There's no one else around when you live that far away from everything else.''

''How can you say you're not a real Fortune?'' she demanded. ''You're as much a Fortune as any of your siblings.''

"You missed the point, Willa. I don't know where I came from. I don't know my roots, and I never will."

"Roots aren't important. It's the tree that everyone sees, and it's the tree that is productive."

"But the roots hold it in place and nourish it. And I don't have any."

"You have as many roots as your brothers and your sister. Yours just got started a little later in your life." Her voice was firm. "Your roots are probably stronger than theirs, in fact. You had to work to develop them. It took a tremendous amount of determination and inner strength to rebound from the kind of beginning you must have had in your life. If you hadn't been a strong person to begin with, that kind of beginning would have destroyed you."

"Willa, I didn't tell you my life story so you would admire me," he said, frustrated.

"Then why did you tell me?"

"So you could see how different I am from you. So you could see the kind of background I came from."

"Are you trying to scare me away?" she demanded.

"Yes," he growled. "I'm not the kind of man you deserve. I'm not like you, Willa."

"I think you're more like me than you want to believe," she said gently. "I think your family means everything to you, and you would do anything for them. I've seen how you've watched over them, particularly Matilda, and I've seen the love on your face when you think no one's looking. I think you work hard at your job, and that it's important to you. You're an honorable man, Griff, and there's nothing in your life story that could make me think otherwise.''

''You don't know what you're talking about,'' he said, shaking his head.

She merely smiled at him. ''Remember how I told you that I learned early to watch and figure out the people around me? I still do. And long before you rescued me at my apartment, I was watching you. I had you figured out before the first time you said hello to me.''

This conversation was getting away from him. He didn't want to hear about how Willa had been watching him for a long time. He didn't want to hear about what she thought of him. And he particularly didn't want to hear that she'd wanted him for a long time. That was coming next. He could see it in her eyes.

''Isn't it about time for bed?'' he asked abruptly.

For a moment she held his gaze steadily. Her eyes told him that she understood what he was doing, understood the desperation that fueled it. Then she nodded slowly. ''I guess so.'' She glanced at the fire. ''Do we have to put the fire out first?''

''I'll leave it going, just in case the generator breaks down again.'' *Or we end up on the floor in front of the fire.*

He put that thought firmly out of his head.

''I'll check the doors and windows,'' he said, jumping out of his seat. He was too edgy to sit still and watch her. He wanted, too badly, to touch her again. So he'd send her to the bedroom, and he'd hide in the loft. He wouldn't sleep for a long, long time, but at least he wouldn't have the temptation of her within arm's reach.

"Thanks," she said, standing. When she stretched, he closed his eyes. Her shirt tightened over her breasts and her jeans outlined her legs and hips. If he looked at her, he would be lost.

"I'll see you in the morning," she said, then closed the bedroom door softly behind her.

He was alone in the room. Thank God. He couldn't have taken much more. For a moment, he seriously considered taking her back to College Station, as she'd wanted to do. At least they wouldn't be trapped in this tiny cabin, with no place to go to escape the tension that simmered between them.

Then he rejected the idea. No matter what the cost to himself, he would protect Willa. He'd promised Ryan, and he'd promised Willa. This cabin was far safer than College Station. So here they would stay.

After checking all the windows and the door one final time, he banked the fire, closed the fireplace screen and turned off the lights. He could hear the generator humming softly outside the cabin. A part of him, a part that appalled him, longed for it to break down again, so that he would have an excuse to get close to Willa.

He swore under his breath as he climbed the stairs to the loft. It was going to be an endless night.

* * *

Willa emerged from the bedroom the next morning to find Griff drinking coffee and listening to the news on the radio. He didn't turn around when her door opened, but she saw his back straighten.

"Good morning," she said.

He turned around—reluctantly, she thought. "Good morning." He looked away quickly, but not before she saw the shadows beneath his eyes. Apparently, he hadn't gotten any more sleep than she had.

"Is there more of that coffee?" she asked brightly.

"I value my life." His voice was dry. "Of course there's more coffee."

She poured herself a cup and took a gulp. She needed something to wake her up. She would need her wits about her this morning.

She knew why Griff had told her his life story. He'd hoped she'd be repulsed by it, be put off by the horrible tale. He'd told her about himself only because he wanted to create some distance between them.

But his story had done just the opposite. It had simply given her another reason to admire Griffin Fortune. He'd struggled back from an appalling childhood to become a strong, honorable man, a man who always did the right thing. A man she cared about.

She refused to think about him as anything more than that. Down that road lay certain heartache. Griff, she knew, didn't want to get involved with her. He was attracted to her. He wanted to make love with her. But that was as far as he would allow himself to go.

And maybe it was better that way. At least, that's what she'd told herself during the long, lonely night.

After taking another scalding gulp of coffee, she set the cup down on the counter, and said, "What excitement do you have planned for today?"

"I'm figuring on a nice, dull day," he said without turning around. "No generator breakdowns, no trips into El Paso, no trucks following us on the road. Dull and boring are the keys to happiness."

"Sounds good to me," she said, gripping her coffee cup more tightly. They had to do something other than sit around the cabin. They would both go mad. Or they'd end up tearing off each other's clothes. She wasn't sure which would be worse. "How are you going to keep yourself occupied?"

"I noticed a few maintenance chores that needed to be done outside. I thought I'd take care of those for Mary Ellen. It's the least I can do."

And it will keep me away from you. The words were unspoken, but they echoed between them in the room. "That's a good idea. I'll see if anything needs to be done inside."

He stood up abruptly. "I'm going to call Ryan tonight. I'll see if he's found anything."

"All right." Clearly, Griff was hoping they'd go back to College Station, and the sooner the better. But her life at the university seemed so far off—more distant than the hours it would take to drive back to her apartment. She'd changed in these few days she'd spent with Griff. Everything she'd thought she knew about herself had shifted and turned upside down. Now she wasn't sure what she wanted from her life.

Griff grabbed his jacket and hurried out the door. He closed it carefully behind him, but she knew it would be hours before she saw him again.

That was just as well, she told herself. She should do something more useful than daydreaming about Griff. She finished her coffee, then poured herself another cup and began to assess what needed to be done to the cabin.

Several hours later the cabin gleamed. Everything had been cleaned, polished and washed, and there was nothing left to do. Griff hadn't been back inside, but she'd heard him throughout the morning, hammering, sawing and pounding on the cabin walls.

Willa stretched and looked outside. The sun was shining and the sky was cloudless, and suddenly she yearned to be outdoors. She slipped into her coat and walked out onto the porch.

It was far warmer than she'd expected. The scent of the pine trees wafted to her, carried on the balmy breeze. It almost felt like spring, although it was close to Christmas. Inhaling deeply, she stood on the porch and let the sun work its magic on her.

Griff walked around the corner of the cabin, stopping short when he saw her. "Is something wrong?"

"No. I just wanted to come outside. It's a glorious day."

He walked up the steps and past her, then set down the can of wood stain he was carrying. "Don't go anywhere that I can't see you."

''I won't,'' she snapped, annoyed at him for ruining her mood by reminding her why they were here. ''I'm not going anywhere.''

He grunted as he applied stain to a new piece of wood on the floor of the porch. She watched him for a moment, then moved to a lower step and sat. The sound of Griff working behind her blended with the whisper of the wind in the trees. Birds fluttered in the pines, and as she listened to their calls and whistles, a quiet peace settled over her. If she closed her eyes, she could imagine that none of the ugliness in College Station had happened. She could imagine she and Griff were a couple, happy to be spending time alone in their secluded cabin.

Deliberately she opened her eyes and drank in reality. She was just setting herself up for disappointment if she started imagining happy scenarios between herself and Griff. He'd made it very plain how he felt.

Cupping her chin in her hand, she stared into the distance. She didn't realize Griff had moved until he dropped down on the stair next to her.

''Did you find a lot to keep you busy inside?'' he asked.

She shook her head. ''Two adults don't make much of a mess. But I cleaned it, anyway. How about you? Did you find many things that needed to be repaired out here?''

''Not much. Mary Ellen keeps the cabin in good shape.''

He stared out at the trees with her, finally rousing

himself to say, "What do you want to do with the rest of the day? It's barely noon."

"Maybe we should try another hike. The weather is too wonderful to stay inside, and I can probably manage not to humiliate myself this time. My head is completely healed, and I'm sure I'm used to the altitude by now."

"We're staying off the mountain," he said firmly. "The rock is too crumbly. I don't want to take any more chances."

"Then what would you like to do?"

Silence hung between them for a moment, heavy with unspoken desires. Suddenly the tension that had eased for a few hours rushed back with a vengeance. Griff stood up and moved away from her.

"Why don't we make some sandwiches and go for a walk?" he said. "When I was out yesterday, I saw a little meadow not too far away. We might as well enjoy the weather while we can. It's supposed to turn colder again tomorrow."

"A picnic sounds like a great idea." Willa jumped up and headed for the house. "I'll get some food together."

Griff didn't follow her into the house, and she was grateful. The kitchen was so small that they would constantly be bumping up against each other, continually touching. And that wouldn't be a smart thing right now.

It took only a few minutes to pack a simple lunch of sandwiches, fruit, and cookies. This time Willa included two bottles of water in the lunch. She remembered how easy it had been to get dehydrated in the dry air.

"Let me carry that," Griff said, when she came back outside. He stashed the bags in his backpack, then swung the pack up onto his back. "Ready to go?"

She nodded. "All set."

They started walking through the trees that surrounded the house, but they veered away from the mountain. "Where did you see this meadow?" she asked.

"I saw it while I was up on the mountain. I wanted to get a better feel for our surroundings, so I made a point of looking all around. This meadow is really just a small area where there aren't any trees, but it looks like it'll have a great view. And we don't have anything better to do than explore."

Willa could think of several better things to do, and she suspected that Griff could, too. But she'd tried to convince herself during the night that she and Griff would both be better off if they didn't get involved. So she plastered a smile on her face and said, "Since we have all this time on our hands, we might as well act as if we're on vacation, right?"

"Right."

He didn't sound as if he were on a carefree vacation, Willa thought, but then, she didn't feel that way, either. The tension between them was becoming a strain, particularly since Griff clearly wanted to stay away from her, and she had decided that would be best. But she could put up a front with the best of them.

So she followed him as he walked through the trees, and tried to keep her mind off the way his jeans fit and the way his wide shoulders moved beneath his shirt.

Ten

It didn't take long to get to Griff's little meadow. And he was right: the view was spectacular. She forgot all about the trouble between them as she stood at the edge of the clearing and gazed out at the magnificence of the mountains surrounding El Paso.

"It's quite a sight, isn't it?" he said softly next to her.

"It's wonderful. I love the area near College Station, but this is breathtaking. I could stand here and just look for hours."

"I thought you would enjoy the view." She heard the satisfaction in his voice. "Come over here. There are a couple of boulders that will make perfect back rests."

He led her closer to the edge, and she saw that the meadow ended at a steep drop-off. Set back from the edge about ten feet was a jumble of large rocks. They looked as if they had been set there deliberately to form a cozy, secluded spot on the edge of the world.

"This is perfect," she said, turning to Griff with a smile.

"I can't take credit for it," he said. "I just saw it from above." He gestured at the mountain that towered above them. "But it does look like a good spot for a picnic."

Griff took a blanket out of his backpack. "I didn't know what the ground would be like," he explained. "I wanted to make sure we had a place to sit."

"That was very thoughtful of you," she said with a grin. "It looks like you're an expert at this picnic stuff."

Instead of scowling at her teasing, as she expected, he surprised her with a smile. "I can manage to be civilized once in a while."

"Can I thank your mother for that?"

"And my sister." He looked nostalgic. "When she was just a kid, she always wanted to tag along with Brody and Reed and me when we worked on the ranch. In order to distract her, we had a lot of picnics. I learned early to bring a blanket, or Mattie would go home looking like she'd rolled in every dirt hole on the ranch. And my mother would be very unhappy."

"I like your sister very much," she said, knowing he would hear the wistful tone in her voice. "I've always wished I had a sister."

"She was a hellion as a kid, but she's grown up pretty well," he said, sounding studiously gruff. "And she seems blissfully happy with Dawson."

"Did you think that both of your brothers and your sister would get married when you came to the U.S.?" she asked, turning to look at him.

"Not a chance," he said immediately. "Reed wasn't looking for any kind of relationship since he'd broken up with his girlfriend. The last thing I expected was that he'd fall in love and get married here. And Brody has been all business for a long time. But I guess he was using his work to hide his disappointment over losing Jillian. I'm glad they found each other again.''

''And you were the one who set Mattie up with Dawson,'' she reminded mischievously.

''Not on purpose.'' He scowled at her. ''I didn't think Dawson even liked Mattie.''

''Apparently he liked her more than you realized.''

''It looks that way. They got off to a rocky start, but she couldn't stop smiling the last time I saw her. I guess that's all that matters.''

''It's going to be hard for you and your parents and brothers to be separated from her, isn't it?'' she asked gently. ''Australia is a long way from Texas.''

''I'll manage to get to Texas pretty often,'' he said. ''I have a fair amount of flexibility in my job. And I suspect my parents will make the trip frequently, too. Especially when the grandchildren start to come along. Now that we're going to have close ties with Ryan and the Fortune businesses, my brothers will all be back and forth between Texas and Australia. So it's not like we'll never see Mattie again.''

''It won't be the same, though.''

He turned and looked out over the mountains that spread in front of them. They looked as if they went on forever. ''Nothing is ever the same, Willa. I figured that out a long time ago. Everything changes. Sure, I'll miss Mattie, and our relationship will be different. But I'm pleased for her and Brody and Reed. It's good to see them all so happy."

"You sound very lonely," she said, without stopping to think.

At that he turned and looked at her. "Why do you say that?"

"You sound like you're on the outside, looking in at your siblings and at a life you can't have."

He stared at her for a moment, then he looked away. "You're very perceptive, Willa. I guess you were right when you said you pay attention to people. I've always felt a little bit like an outsider with my family. I'm different from them. There's always a part of me that I have to hold back, a part of me I can't share. I've never told them the details about my job."

"You're trying to protect them," she said. "Maybe they don't want protecting."

"It's more than that. I'm trying to protect myself, too."

Willa wrapped her arms around her knees and rested her head there. "You're not that little boy sleeping under the bush anymore. You don't have to protect yourself from your own family."

"Maybe *protect* was the wrong word. I guess I don't want to disillusion them. I don't want them to think less of me. And they would if they knew what I do."

"I don't think you're giving them enough credit." She turned her head so she could watch him. "They worry about you, Griff. I've heard Mattie talking about your job. They're frightened for you. I think they need to know the details. And nothing you can say will make me believe they'll think less of you if they know what you do. They love you."

She took a deep breath and touched his arm. His muscles were as hard as the rock they leaned against. "Your parents and your siblings know what kind of man you are, Griff. They know you're an honorable person. Tell them what you do."

There was silence as Griff stared out at the vista. "You make it sound so simple," he finally said. "And I know it isn't simple."

"Why not? Most things are simple, if you cut to the heart of the matter."

To her surprise, his lips curled into a faint smile. "I'm not sure if you're good or bad for me, Willa. But you make me think. Maybe you're right. Maybe I do need to tell them about my job."

"They're always going to worry. But I think they'd worry less if they knew more about what you do."

"I'll think about it."

She shifted on the ground and grabbed for her courage. "I know what kind of person you are, too, Griff. Nothing you could tell me would change how I feel about you."

He turned to meet her gaze. "You know far less about me than you think you know." His voice was flat.

"You're wrong. I've spent several days with you now, and I've seen all I need to see. You're a good man, Griff, even if you don't want to think so. You may do a tough job, but that doesn't change the kind of person you are, deep inside. And that's all that counts.''

She saw something that looked like wonder in the golden-brown depths of his eyes. "You really believe that, don't you?"

"Yes," she said, and her voice rang with conviction. "Absolutely."

He shook his head. "I don't want to disillusion you."

"You never could. You told me you would protect me, and you have. Even though you really didn't know me, you dropped everything to keep me safe." She plunged ahead. "You won't even touch me, because that might distract you from your job. Even though I want you to touch me."

"These are unnatural circumstances," he said, and his voice was harsh. "You wouldn't feel that way if we hadn't been thrown together like this."

"That's not true. I've been fascinated by you since the first time we met."

"I'm fascinated by the snakes at the zoo, but that doesn't mean I want to get in the cage with them. You're attracted to me because I'm so different from you."

"You're not giving me much credit," she said, and she struggled to keep her voice even. "Don't you think I can see beyond the superficial differences between us? We're a lot more alike than you want to think we are."

He swiveled to face her, and now he was so close she could feel the heat from his body surrounding her.

In his eyes she could see denial, but beneath that was a glimmer of hope. "We're as different as two people can be," he said evenly.

She focused on the glimmer. "We're not, Griff, and I think that's why you're so determined not to get close to me. You can see that we're alike. We're both lonely, even though we both have lots of people who love us. We both grew up thinking we never really belonged. And we spend far too much of our lives on the outside, looking in."

"Even if what you're saying is true, that doesn't change anything."

"Why not?"

"Because I'm no good for a woman like you," he said roughly.

"What kind of woman is that?"

"You're a good person," he said. "You're kind and gentle. You're a lady. And I don't even know my real name."

"Your real name is Griffin Fortune," she said, leaning forward to face him, her voice full of heat. "Your real name has been Griffin Fortune since your father found you under that bush."

"What I do for a living is a dirty job."

She could see that he was fighting this. She leaned closer to him. "You're doing a job that needs to be done. Someone has to do it. And everyone is glad that someone does."

He shook his head slowly. "You're something else, Willa. What would your father say if he saw you with a man like me?"

She felt her mouth curl slowly upward. "He'd say I'd made a damn good choice for myself."

"Don't give me that." His voice was stern. "He wanted to see you settled with someone who could give you the kind of life you deserve—someone with a stable job, someone who wouldn't drag you all around the world with him."

"He wanted me to be happy," she said. "My father would have recognized you for the kind of man you are. He would have liked you. And he would have respected you."

Slowly he reached for her. "You make it impossible for me to resist you, Willa," he whispered. "God knows, I've tried to do the right thing. I've tried to stay away from you. But I want you too much. I've wanted you from the first moment I saw you. I never dreamed that you would want me, too."

"I haven't thought of much besides you since the first time I saw you." She couldn't believe how bold she was being—demure Willa Simms, who had always done what was expected of her. "I didn't mind living at Ryan's ranch while they were decorating my apartment, because you would show up once in a while."

"And whenever I did, I tried to stay away from you." He reached out and twined his hand with hers.

"I know. I figured you weren't interested in a mousy college professor."

"I was interested. And you're not mousy, Willa," he whispered, leaning closer. "You're beautiful."

He reached out and wrapped his hands around her

shoulders, pulling her closer. Her heart raced, and blood roared in her ears as she watched his eyes darken. "I'm going to kiss you," he murmured. "And once I kiss you, I'm not going to want to stop."

"I don't want you to stop," she said, hardly recognizing the throaty, sexy voice as her own.

His eyes blazed, then he crushed her mouth beneath his. He didn't seduce her with easy, gentle kisses. He didn't go slowly, trying to convince her. He possessed her, taking and claiming her as his own. For just a moment, his hunger was uncontrolled, and she felt the wildness that he usually kept so deeply hidden.

Then his mouth gentled on hers. He nipped at her lower lip, then outlined its shape with his tongue. When her breath hitched, he slipped into her mouth to taste and tempt her.

She wound her arms around his neck and tried to bring him closer. With an inarticulate murmur, he eased her down on the blanket and stretched out next to her. "I knew there was a good reason to bring this blanket," he whispered in her ear. His breath rippled through her hair and caressed her skin, making her shiver.

He pulled her closer, warming her with the heat of his body. Then he found her mouth again. He lingered there for a long time, tasting and teasing. Desire coiled inside her, making her shiver again. Restlessly she let her hands roam his back, lingering over every taut muscle, every ridge in his spine.

When she slipped her hands beneath his shirt to touch his hot skin, he groaned into her mouth. "You

set me on fire,'' he muttered against her neck. He
tensed when she touched his hard belly, and flinched
when she let her fingers drift toward the waistband of
his jeans.

"I want you to touch me,'' he whispered, moving
away from her hands. "But not yet. I want to spend
hours touching you.''

He slowly unbuttoned her shirt, letting the cool air
drift over her skin. But when he unsnapped her bra
and covered her breasts with his hands, heat flooded
her again.

He groaned again, deep in his throat, then lowered
his head to take her nipple in his mouth. She arched
against him, a hot need filling her body. "Griff,'' she
gasped.

Again, he covered her mouth with his, swallowing
her soft cries while he circled her nipples with his
thumbs. She twisted against him, needing to be closer,
wanting to pull away the barriers of their clothing.

Blindly she reached for the button on his jeans, but
he took her hand and held it. "Wait, Willa.''

Slowly she opened her eyes. He stared down at her,
his face flushed with passion, his eyes burning into
her. "Wait for what?''

"I want to make love with you. But not here. I
don't have any protection with me.''

Her face flooded with heat. "I didn't think of that
at all,'' she whispered. Was she so swept away by
desire that she would have forgotten something so
important?

"I have some back at the cabin.'' He swept her

into his arms again and kissed her. "Why don't we go back?"

"Yes," she said, and sat up. Her shirt fluttered open, and she pulled it hastily together. Griff reached out and rebuttoned it, and her heart speeded up when she saw that his hands weren't quite steady.

"Let's go." He quickly stuffed the blanket back into his pack and slung it over his shoulder. Then he took her hand and they headed back through the trees.

Neither of them spoke as they walked to the cabin. Desire still hummed along her nerves, making her shaky and weak. Griff looked everywhere but at her. When they reached the edge of the clearing, he squeezed her hand, then let her go. "Wait here for a minute. I'll be right back."

He disappeared around the corner of the cabin, then reappeared less than a minute later. Taking her hand, he gave her a smile. "Everything's okay."

But when they walked into the cabin and locked the door behind them, he didn't sweep her into his arms immediately. Instead, he took her hand and led her over to the couch by the fireplace.

"What's wrong?" she asked, because she saw in his face that something was.

"Nothing's wrong," he said slowly. "But there are some things you need to know before we make love."

"I know all I need to know about you." She took his hand. "Nothing else matters."

"I want to tell you about my job." He held on to her hand, but he didn't look at her. "You were right earlier. I owe it to my family to tell them, and I owe it to you. You have a right to know what I do, Willa.''

''You don't have to tell me if you'd rather not. It's not going to make any difference in how I feel about you.''

At that he did turn to look at her, and his face was somber. ''Don't say that until you hear what I have to tell you.''

''All right, tell me about your job.'' She settled back against the cushions of the couch, but she didn't let go of his hand.

He looked away and stared at the fireplace and the ashes of their fire from the night before. ''I work for British Intelligence,'' he said after a moment. ''I'm what they call a covert investigator. I work under-cover, sometimes for months at a time. My job is to infiltrate groups that we consider dangerous and ex-tract information from them.''

''It sounds very dangerous.''

''It's a dirty, ugly job,'' he said. ''Do you under-stand what it is that I do? I make people believe I'm their friend, that I believe in their cause, and then I betray them. I watch them get arrested and sometimes I watch them get killed. And I've killed people myself when I've had to.''

She stared at him for a moment, then she reached out and touched his face. ''And how many deaths have you prevented?'' she finally asked.

''That's not the point—''

''Yes, it is the point. We all want to live in free-dom, to take our democracies for granted. But we can't do that unless there are people like you, willing to risk their lives to keep the rest of us safe. If there weren't people like you, we'd be at the mercy of every fanatic in the world, every fringe group with a grudge. We would live with fear every moment of every day. I don't know why you feel you're dirty or tainted,'' she said, her voice fierce. ''The rest of us should be thanking you for what you do, every single day that we wake up in a free country.''

Slowly he shook his head, but the lines on his face had eased. ''You're choosing not to understand.''

''I understand just fine. I'm sure that some of the things you do are ugly and would horrify me. I'm sure you could tell me things that would give me nightmares for months. But I'm just as sure that you're a good man, and an honorable one. Your job isn't going to change the way I feel about you. I'm proud of you for what you do.''

The hardness disappeared from his eyes. He cupped her head in his hands and leaned forward to kiss her. ''You're too good to be true, Willa. I'm going to have to hold onto you tightly, to make sure you don't disappear on me.''

''I'm not going anywhere, Fortune. And you can take that to the bank.''

He grinned. ''I suspect that's American slang. But I think I like the sound of it.''

He bent to kiss her again, and she wrapped her arms around him and pulled him closer. His kiss tasted of desperation, and she knew he expected her to turn away from him. Not only did they come from different countries, they came from different worlds. She knew nothing about the shadowy, dangerous world he inhabited. And he was about as far from a college professor as he could be. Logically, sensibly, she and Griff didn't belong together.

But she wasn't feeling very sensible. And Griff's arms around her, his mouth on hers, made her feel as if she'd finally come home.

She had always been cautious and careful, both in her personal and professional life. She had always believed that relationships developed slowly, with care and nurturing. But she had never felt this wild need before. No one had ever stirred her blood the way Griff did. She had never wanted anyone more.

"Let me make love with you," he murmured into her mouth. "Let me touch you and taste you and lose myself in you."

She leaned back and opened her eyes and saw the need in his face. "Yes."

He rose from the couch and scooped her up into his arms, then carried her into the bedroom. He let her slide down the length of his body, then he yanked back the quilt from the bed. She reached up to unbutton her blouse, but he gently drew her hands away.

"Not yet." He kissed her palms, his mouth lingering until she trembled, then he gently let her go. "Don't move. I'll be right back."

He hurried out of the room, returning in a moment to set a handful of foil packets on the table next to the bed. She stared at them, then looked at Griff, a slow smile gracing her mouth. "I like the way you think."

"I've wanted you for a long time, Willa."

He fisted the material of her blouse in his hands and bent to kiss the hollow above her collarbone. When she shivered in response, he began to unbutton her blouse. It fell away with a whisper, and he moved his mouth slowly down to her chest. Her bra disappeared next, then he feathered his hands across her breasts.

Desire speared her, sharp and hot and urgent. She reached out and unbuttoned his shirt with shaking fingers, pulling it away from his shoulders. His skin was hot and smooth, and the muscles beneath were taut. When her fingers fumbled with the fly of his jeans, he gently pushed her hands away. "Let me."

His jeans dropped to the floor, and she stared at him, moved by the powerful beauty of his body. Then he knelt in front of her and unbuttoned her jeans, kissing her thighs, then her calves, as the rough denim slid down her legs. By the time she was naked, she ached with the need to feel him inside her.

He slid onto the bed next to her, and when she touched him, he tensed and closed his eyes. After a moment, he groaned and moved her hand away. "I'm going to explode if you keep doing that. And I've waited too long for you to let that happen." He rolled over and kissed her, pinning her hands to the bed. "You can play all you want later."

"I'll hold you to that."

"You can hold anything you want. Later."

He covered her mouth with his, and she lost herself in his kiss. When he cupped her with his hand, she moaned his name and moved against him. "I need you, Griff. I can't wait any longer."

"Willa." He rose above her, then took her mouth in another devouring kiss. When she strained to meet him, he slid into her, filling her and claiming her.

They moved together, their hands clasped, their mouths clinging together, completely joined. Sensation bloomed and grew until it filled her completely. When the first wave crashed over her, she wrapped her arms around him and held him tightly, whispering his name. And when he shuddered against her, the only sound she heard was his, murmuring her name.

Griff waited until his breathing returned to normal, waited until the world stopped spinning, then he shifted to the side and gathered Willa close to him. She murmured contentedly and burrowed her head into his neck.

"Are you all right?" he asked, when she didn't move.

Finally she lifted her head and looked at him. "I'm not sure. Am I still alive?"

The stunned expression in her eyes eased the sudden vise around his heart. "Let's check you out." He smoothed his hand down her back and shaped her hips and buttocks. Her satiny skin sliding against his palm made him stir again. "You feel more than alive. You make me feel alive."

Her hand fluttered against his back, and she tightened her hold on him. ''I had no idea,'' she said, and her voice sounded stunned, too.

Tenderness filled him, and he kissed her again. ''Maybe we should try that again so you can be sure.''

She raised her head to look at him, and slowly she smiled. ''Maybe we should. I'm trained to observe, you know. But I need plenty of data to support my conclusions.''

''I've got all the data you can handle.''

Eleven

Weak morning sunlight streamed in the window when Griff woke up the next day. Without thinking, he moved closer to Willa. She lay curled up next to him, her face against his chest, one hand resting on his leg. She looked vulnerable and innocent as she slept beside him.

He pulled the sheet up to cover her, then rolled over and stared at the ceiling. In spite of what she'd told him, in spite of the way she'd touched him and tasted him and made love with him, he still felt as if he'd robbed her of some of her innocence.

He didn't care what she'd said. Willa didn't belong with a man like him. And sooner or later, she would realize it. His heart contracted, but he forced himself to face the truth. Sooner or later, she would come to her senses and return to her safe, unstained world.

But he would enjoy the time they had left. Another surge of wanting came over him as he looked at Willa, sleeping beside him. They had made love several times during the night, but his need for her was just as fierce, just as powerful as it had been before he'd touched her. And if her reactions were any indication, she felt the same way.

He rolled over and pulled her close to him, kissing the top of her tousled head. Sleepily she smiled up at him.

"Hi, there."

"Hi, yourself." He brushed a kiss over her mouth, then sat up, ignoring the need that gripped him. "How about some food? I think we skipped a meal or two yesterday, and I want to make sure you keep up your strength."

"That sounds wonderful." She reached for the sheet, holding it in front of her as she sat up in the bed. A delicate pink suffused her cheeks.

"It's too late for the sheet," he said, his voice solemn as he tried to hide a grin. He felt younger than he had in years. "I've already seen all there is to see."

She stuck her tongue out at him. "No gentleman would point that out to me."

"I never claimed to be a gentleman." He bent over and kissed her thoroughly, then stood. "Why don't you take a shower? I'm going to call Ryan and find out if he's made any progress."

The laughter disappeared from her eyes. "All right."

She moved to get out of bed, but he put his hand on her arm. "Wait, Willa."

Slowly she turned to face him. "What?" He saw that she was hurt, and cursed himself for his insensitivity.

"I want nothing more than to forget about Ryan, forget about what happened in College Station, and stay here with you.'' He leaned forward and kissed her, desire stirring hot and fierce once again. ''Can you have any doubts about that?''

''I hope that's true,'' she murmured against his lips.

He leaned back and smiled. ''You can take that to the bank,'' he said, quoting her own words back to her. ''But I need to call Ryan. He's going to wonder why I haven't contacted him. And I said earlier that I was going to call him last night, remember?''

''Yes, you did.'' Slowly the pain disappeared from her eyes. ''But can I hope he hasn't heard anything yet?''

''You can. And I do, too.'' He was selfish enough to want a little more time with her before the world intruded. ''Go ahead and take a shower while I call him, then we'll make some breakfast.''

''And after breakfast?'' she said, a spark of mischief in her eyes again.

''I saw a few games in one of the cabinets,'' he said, hiding another grin. ''I'm sure we can find a way to amuse ourselves.''

She laughed and climbed out of bed, dragging the sheet with her. ''I'm sure we can, Fortune. I'll think about the kind of games we'll play while I'm in the shower.''

He watched her walk to the bathroom, relishing the view from the rear as the sheet gaped open. When the door shut behind her, he grabbed his jeans from the floor and went into the other room to pick up the phone.

Lounging on the couch, he dialed the number of Ryan's private phone line, the one that went directly to his office. He knew Ryan would be in his home office already, hard at work. After only a couple of rings, Ryan picked up the phone and said, "Fortune here."

"Ryan, it's Griff," he answered. "I wanted to check in with you, let you know that everything is all right at this end. Have you learned anything in College Station?"

"We haven't learned one damn thing." Ryan's voice was filled with frustration. "I've got investigators combing the town, but they haven't turned up the van, or any other information. And there's no sign of Clint, either. It's like those two painters vanished into thin air."

Griff fought down the relief that overwhelmed him. "That's too bad, Ryan."

"Yeah, well, we're doing all we can," his uncle answered gruffly. "I'm glad to hear that you're safe in the cabin."

"Not a hint of trouble," Griff answered. "A belt broke on the generator, but we managed to get it going again."

"Were there spare parts in the shed?"

"No, but we found one in town. After this is over, you might want to tell Mary Ellen to have someone check it thoroughly."

"She has someone in El Paso who services the cabin regularly. I'll mention it to her."

"Don't say anything until after we leave," Griff warned his uncle.

"I know that, Griff." Ryan sighed. "I'm sorry to leave you and Willa stranded in the cabin, but I don't want to take any chances. I'm hoping we find something soon."

"Don't worry about us," Griff said quickly. "Willa is safe, and that's all that matters."

"Thanks, Griff. I owe you for this."

"It's my pleasure," he replied. "Call if there's any news."

"I'll do that."

They said goodbye, and Griff hung up the phone.

When he returned to the bedroom, he heard the shower running and he smiled. Pulling off his jeans, he opened the bathroom door.

Betsy Keene eased away from Ryan Fortune's office door as she heard him set the phone back in the receiver. Her heart raced and she knew her cheeks were flushed, but she forced herself to continue dusting as she moved steadily away from the office. If Ryan came out, or if anyone else came along, it had to look as if she were merely doing her job.

Ryan had been talking to Griffin Fortune, that nephew of his from Australia. Ryan had called him by name. And they'd been talking about a cabin near El Paso. Was Griffin the one who'd rescued Willa? Was he keeping her in the cabin?

Betsy's mind raced as she worked, slowly and methodically. This could be the information that Clint had been waiting for. This could be the breakthrough that he'd wanted.

As she moved farther away from the office, a part of Betsy prayed that the information would mean nothing to Clint. Her lover meant to harm Willa Simms, she was sure of it. And she had a soft spot for Willa.

But she would tell Clint what she'd heard. She'd promised him she would, after all. Her promises hadn't seemed to matter to Clint, though. He had only become more moody and angry since they failed to shoot Matilda and failed to kidnap Willa. Ever since the night he'd raged at her in the tiny trailer, he'd been unpredictable and frightening. She didn't want to think about what he would do if he ever did find Willa Simms.

The day passed much too quickly, even though she did several small additional jobs to put off the inevitable confrontation with Clint. Finally she could delay no longer, and she drove slowly home to the trailer she had shared with him ever since his escape from prison.

Her heart sank when she saw the bottle of beer on the table next to the couch. Clint was always more unreasonable when he had been drinking. But she gathered her courage and closed the door behind her.

"I heard something at work today," she said with exaggerated brightness as she went into the kitchen to start dinner. "I overheard Ryan talking to Griffin Fortune. He's one of the nephews from Australia."

"I know who he is." Clint's voice was low and

deadly behind her. "He's another one who's taking what should be mine."

"He's not at the ranch right now," Betsy said hastily. "But I think maybe he's with Willa Simms."

Clint jumped to his feet. "What did you hear?"

"Ryan was talking to him on the phone. He mentioned a cabin, and he mentioned El Paso. Does that mean anything to you?"

She held her breath, hoping that it wouldn't. She didn't want to think about what Clint might do to Willa. Or to Griff, who had apparently outmaneuvered him at Willa's apartment.

But a smile slowly spread over Clint's face. His eyes glittered, and he nodded with satisfaction. "My sister Mary Ellen owns a cabin in the mountains near El Paso. I know just where it is." His smile grew wider. "I should have thought of that cabin myself."

"Do you think that's where Willa is?" Betsy asked timidly.

Clint laughed, and the sound sent shivers up Betsy's spine. "I'll bet on it. In fact, I'll stake my future on it." He turned his gaze on her. "And yours."

"What are you going to do, Clint?" She wiped her damp palms on her dress. If he went to the cabin by himself, she thought wildly, maybe she could warn Ryan.

The disloyal thought shocked her, but she was chilled by the fear of what Clint would do to Willa. And to her, she admitted to herself.

"*We're* going to take a trip to El Paso," Clint said,

picking up his beer bottle and taking a long pull. "We'll leave bright and early tomorrow morning. You can call in sick to work." He took another drink, and Betsy saw with despair that madness glittered in his eyes again. "We have work to do in El Paso."

Willa woke up and looked over at Griff. He was still sound asleep. His brown hair stuck up straight on his head, and there were no signs of the tense lines that usually grooved his face. He looked relaxed and happy, and Willa grinned.

What they had been doing for the past two days would make anyone relaxed and happy.

She couldn't remember ever being so content. Although she knew it was irresponsible, she hoped that it took a long, long time for Ryan to find out who had tried to kidnap her. Her world had narrowed to include only Griff.

Her friends, her home and her career in College Station seemed like part of another life, one that didn't belong to her. She thought back with amazement on her days at the university last fall. She had only been half alive then, she realized, only existing. There had been no colors in her life before Griff.

And now her days and nights were filled with magic.

Her smile faded as she slipped out of the bed. She hoped that magic would still crackle between them when they left the cabin. Sooner or later, they would have to return to the real world. And she was frightened of what would happen between them.

Griff, she knew, was still wary of their relationship. Although she knew that their lovemaking moved him deeply, she suspected he still felt that he wasn't good enough for her. When he didn't think she was looking, he would have a sad, brooding expression on his face. Almost, she thought, as if he were imagining what life was going to be like after he left her in College Station.

She didn't want to think about that. She didn't want to think at all about life without Griff. Just a few short months ago, she'd thought her job was the most important thing in the world. Now it was just a way to earn a living. Griff was far more important to her than the prestige of being a professor at the university.

He wouldn't accept that, she knew. He would be horrified at the thought. But there were other universities in the world. And she was well-qualified.

Stunned at the direction her thoughts were taking, Willa slipped on her jeans and a T-shirt, then slid her feet into her shoes. She needed to eat, and so did Griff. Then maybe she could think more rationally about their relationship, and put these crazy thoughts out of her mind. How could she be thinking of throwing away everything she had worked so hard to attain?

Before she stepped out of the room she looked at Griff, and her heart constricted. She wouldn't be throwing anything away, she reminded herself. She would simply be making a new start somewhere else. Because when she looked at the man she loved, her job faded into insignificance.

She *loved* Griff. She could allow herself to admit that now, in the quiet of the cabin, while Griff slept. He wasn't yet ready to hear it, so for now it would be her secret. She hugged it to her heart and smiled as she began to make sandwiches. She and Griff would have another picnic, she thought. After all, they'd never gotten around to eating their sandwiches up on the mountain two days ago.

But this one would be a little more intimate than the last one. For starters, neither of them would be wearing any clothes. And she wasn't even sure they would do much eating.

Smiling to herself and humming a romantic song, she finished making the sandwiches just as a knock sounded at the door of the cabin. Dropping the knife she'd been using, she went to the window and looked outside into the early evening darkness. A beat-up sedan sat in the driveway, empty. And on the porch, standing in front of the door, was a middle-aged woman.

She was short and slender, almost fragile looking. Her brown hair hung limply around her face, and her eyes were frightened. She must be lost, Willa thought, and headed for the door. She almost called Griff, but decided not to wake him. They hadn't gotten a lot of sleep the night before. Or the night before that, she thought, a smile teasing her lips.

A small, lost, middle-aged woman couldn't be a threat to her.

She opened the door a crack, bracing it with her

foot so she could shut it quickly. "Can I help you?" she asked politely.

"I hope so. I must have gotten turned around, because I seem to be lost. Could you tell me how to get back to the main road?"

Willa stared at the woman as fear rose in her throat. Her heart pounded and her palms became slippery with sweat. She opened her mouth to call Griff, but no sound would come out. *She recognized that voice.*

One of the painters in the hallway of her apartment had spoken to her the night she had been abducted. The fog cleared from her memory, and she remembered—

"Griff!"

Her scream echoed off the walls of the cabin as she tried to close the door. But the door wouldn't close. It slammed open, and a man grabbed her with rough hands. She struggled as he held a foul-smelling cloth over her face, but she felt herself getting dizzy and weak.

She fought hard, clawing and scratching and writhing in his arms, but his grip was like iron. She kicked out at the man as she felt herself being pulled out of the cabin, but the world was whirling around her. The last thing she heard was Griff calling her name as she faded into unconsciousness.

Griff woke with a start, then came instantly awake as he realized that Willa had screamed. He jumped out of bed and ran into the living room. The door stood open, but Willa wasn't anywhere in sight.

He ran out the door at full speed, just in time to see two people dumping Willa's limp body into the back seat of a car. As he leaped off the porch and ran toward it, the car took off down the road with a squeal of tires. Realizing he wasn't going to catch it, he memorized the license plate number, then ran back into the cabin, tripping over a woman's brown wig.

After throwing on his clothes, he grabbed his gun and ran back outside, cursing himself. He had let them take Willa. Cold dread settled in the pit of his stomach.

He tried to block the fear from his mind, tried to concentrate only on what had to be done, but he couldn't block his feelings. Willa was in danger, unconscious and probably hurt, and a cold pool of despair froze in his gut.

It was his fault.

If it was the last thing he did, he'd catch the two people who had her, he vowed. He'd follow them to the ends of the earth, if necessary.

He sped over the ruts in the track that led away from the cabin. The car that had taken Willa wasn't far ahead of him, and he had the advantage of knowing the area. He might be able to catch up with it.

He drove faster than he should have, jamming on the brakes when he reached the end of the road that led to the cabin. Which way would they have turned?

After thinking for a moment, he turned toward El Paso. Kidnappers would want anonymity. And a large city was the best place to blend into the background. If the kidnappers turned in the other direction, they would drive for miles without finding another town. They would be conspicuous, and that was the last thing they would want.

Once on the blacktop, Griff accelerated far beyond the speed limit, praying that a police officer would stop him for speeding so he could enlist the officer's help. But he didn't see any other vehicle on the road.

He had almost decided that the kidnappers must have gone the other way when he saw taillights, far ahead of him. Immediately he switched off his headlights, then pressed on the accelerator again.

He crept closer, managing to stay far enough behind the car that the occupants wouldn't be able to see him in the darkness. He was almost sure it was the same car that had disappeared with Willa inside, but he didn't dare get close enough to check the license plate.

As he drove through the night he struggled to banish his fear and focus only on the job he needed to do. He called upon every bit of his training, all his instincts, to think objectively, to make some sort of rational plan.

But his fear for Willa was a living thing, eating away at his mind. It lingered in the air around him, infecting all his thoughts, driving him to push the accelerator to the floor.

When he realized that he had gotten too close to the car in front of him, he braked abruptly. It was too dark for them to see him but the shock cleared some of the fog of rage and despair from his mind.

"Focus, Fortune," he said savagely. "Do you want

to save her, or do you want to feel sorry for yourself?''

He hung back for a few miles, following the taillights but the car ahead of him didn't slow down or speed up. It continued on the road, holding a steady speed. When he'd gotten too close, he'd been able to see two people in the front seat of the car. He'd seen them throw Willa into the back seat, so he assumed she was unconscious and still lying there. He refused to consider any other possibilities.

''If they'd wanted to kill her, they would have done it at the cabin,'' he reminded himself. They didn't have to take her away if all they wanted was to murder her.

So he had to assume she was still alive. And terrified, if she had woken up. Instinctively he pressed the accelerator again, but he caught himself in time. It wouldn't help Willa if her abductors realized he was following them.

As he crested another hill, he saw the lights of El Paso in the distance. If they intended to take her there, as he suspected, it would be easier to follow them. He could get close to them and blend into traffic.

Griff could follow anyone through a city without being spotted. It was a basic skill in the shadowy world in which he worked. He would blend in with all the other vehicles on the road, following them effortlessly until they finally stopped. Unless the kidnappers were professionals, they would never know he was behind them.

But how did the kidnappers find them? he wondered uneasily. Maybe they were professionals. Ryan was the only one who knew where Griff had taken Willa, and he wouldn't tell a soul. He wouldn't even tell his family. They'd agreed on that the first time he'd talked to his uncle. There would be no chance of a leak.

He forced himself to block Willa from his mind as they got closer to El Paso. He would need all his attention to follow the car ahead of him without being seen. But without warning, the car turned abruptly off the road and headed into what looked like a pasture.

Griff approached the area cautiously, then saw that there was a narrow dirt road next to a barbed wire fence. He waited until the car was well ahead of him, then he started down the tracks.

He didn't see anything in the distance. It looked as if they were headed for the mountains, and fear gripped him again. Was Willa dead, after all? Were they looking for a place to dispose of her body?

He kept some distance behind the car. He caught occasional glimpses of the sedan as the road twisted and turned, then it disappeared completely.

A few minutes later he spotted a small building in the middle of the pasture. It appeared run-down and deserted, until suddenly a light flickered inside the building. He stopped the truck and watched as a small figure walked out the door, and a few moments later two people carried a third person inside.

It had to be Willa.

He eased the truck into gear again and drove as close to the building as he dared. Sound would carry for a long way in the clear air. When he could go no farther, he parked the truck so that it blocked the road, then slipped out the door. Easing his gun out of its holster, he headed for the small building.

There was no place inside him for fear or anger. He closed down the part of his mind that was full of Willa, and allowed his instincts to guide him. This was his job, after all. And he was very good at it.

He didn't make a sound as he approached the building. He checked the door silently, finding that they hadn't bothered to lock it. He smiled grimly to himself. They were arrogant and careless. It would make his job easier.

As he crept up to the tiny window, he could hear voices inside. It sounded like a man and a woman, and he thought they were arguing. The woman's voice sounded fearful, and the man sounded triumphant.

We'll see how long that lasts, he thought to himself viciously. He would save Willa, no matter what.

Twelve

Griff eased toward the window to peer inside and assess the situation before he made his move. The two people in the room had their backs to the window. Willa lay on the floor, her hands and feet tightly bound. But her chest rose and fell regularly. She was alive.

And he would make sure she stayed that way.

Her eyes were closed, but as he watched her, he realized that she practically vibrated with tension. She wasn't unconscious, he was certain. She must be faking unconsciousness in order to outwit her captors.

As he looked at her, lying on the hard dirt floor, a wave of admiration and warmth flooded him. He refused to call it anything else. Willa was strong and smart, and she was doing her best to survive

He would die for her, if necessary. Willa was more important to him than his own life.

Willa was safe for the moment, so he transferred his focus to her captors. He needed to find out all he could about the people who had taken her.

"…then we'll call Ryan." The man's tone was vicious. "He'll change his tune once he hears we have his precious goddaughter."

"What about the man who was with her, Clint?" the woman asked timidly. "Don't you think he might come after us?"

"How is he going to find us?" Scorn dripped from the man's voice. "That's why we took the time to find this place. No one would dream of looking here. Even the people who own this ranch have probably forgotten all about this building."

So Clint Lockhart was the kidnapper, Griff thought. He remembered Ryan talking about the man, and the fact that he had escaped from prison. Ryan had been right to be concerned, he thought grimly. Clint had indeed had some mischief planned.

As he listened to Clint rage about how Ryan was going to pay for all the injuries he'd inflicted on Clint, Griff realized that this was the man who was responsible for the attack on his sister Matilda. Deadly cold anger grew inside him. Mattie had escaped injury, but now Lockhart had Willa.

"Are we going to wait here until we get the ransom from Ryan?" the woman asked timidly. Griff wondered who she was. She seemed frightened of Lockhart, which only proved that she was at least a little intelligent.

"I'm going to call Ryan in a few minutes and give him his instructions. I want to listen to the high and mighty Ryan Fortune crawl to me. Then we'll proceed with the next step." Clint laughed, and Griff realized how mad he really was. Apparently the woman did, too, because she shrank away from him.

Clint's laughter stopped suddenly, and his eyes

flashed at the woman. "What's the matter, Betsy? Are you losing your nerve?"

"No, Clint. I just can't wait to start our new life together." She moved farther away from him as she spoke.

Clint smiled, but Griff saw the calculation in his eyes. "And we'll do just that once we tie up a few loose ends."

Lockhart intended to kill both Willa and his accomplice—Griff could see the anticipation in his eyes. He might not even wait until he had the ransom money he was clearly expecting to get from Ryan Fortune. Watching him, listening to him, Griff knew that revenge against the Fortunes was far more important to Clint than anything else.

Griff couldn't wait any longer. He had to surprise Lockhart now. Griff picked up a rock and threw it onto the roof of the shack, aiming for the rear of the building. Clint tensed and spun around, shouting at Betsy, "What was that?"

Clint's back was to the door, and there wouldn't be a better time to surprise the couple. Griff held his gun away from him, and, shoulder to the door, burst into the tiny shack.

He leaped for the older man and knocked him down, but madness gave Clint an unexpected strength, and Griff didn't get a chance to subdue him. Clint rolled over and reached around to his back. When Griff saw the glint of metal, he kicked the other man's hand and sent the gun flying. Clint leaped at him, clawing at his face, but Griff landed a blow to his head that sent Clint reeling. Griff hit him again, and Clint crumpled to the ground, unconscious.

He looked over at the woman, who was cowering over Willa. "Move away from her," he barked. "And keep your hands in the air, where I can see them."

She jumped to obey him, and Griff finally turned to Willa. He needed to secure Lockhart, but not before he made sure Willa was all right. Her eyes were open and she was staring at him, shocked.

"Are you all right?" he asked, dropping to his knees beside her. He skimmed his hands over her face and let his fingers linger. "Did they hurt you at all?"

"I'm fine, I think," she said, but her voice was shaky. "They knocked me out with some horrible-tasting liquid on a rag, but other than that, I'm okay."

He eased her onto her side, then struggled to untie her hands. The ropes were cruelly tight, and her hands were red and beginning to swell. "Your hands are going to hurt when I get these ropes off," he said.

"I can deal with a little pain." She tried to smile. "In fact, I can deal with anything, now that you're here."

He had just tossed aside the rope that bound her hands together when he saw Betsy bend down and pick up the gun he had kicked away from Clint. She pointed it toward him, and he threw himself on top of Willa.

The sound of the gunshot echoed in the small shack, and he waited to feel the burning pain. But there was no pain. Slowly he raised his head. Betsy stood frozen, just feet away from him, a horrified look on her face.

"He was going to kill you," she whispered.

He turned around and saw that Betsy had shot Clint Lockhart. Griff scrambled to check his pulse. The man was dead, but he still held a gun.

"He always carried an extra gun," Betsy said, her voice sounding stunned. "He woke up and pulled it out. He was aiming it at you. I had to shoot him."

"You did the right thing, Betsy." Griff tried to make his voice gentle. "You saved both Willa and me. And probably yourself."

At that the woman turned to him. There was confusion on her face. "I don't know what went wrong. I never wanted to hurt Clint. We were so happy together. I loved him."

"Clint wanted to hurt Willa," Griff said, untying Willa's feet. "Why did he want to do that?"

"He hated Ryan Fortune." She twisted her hands together. "He blamed the Fortunes for taking his family's ranch—said that Ryan's dad stole it from the Lockharts. And he said that Ryan framed him and railroaded him to prison for murdering Sophia."

"None of that is true," Griff said. His arm circled Willa, but he watched Betsy. He had to make sure she wasn't a threat. "Put the gun down, Betsy. No one else is going to get hurt."

She immediately set the gun on the floor, and he reached over and picked it up. "We need to call the police," he said, covering Clint's body with his coat.

Betsy collapsed onto the floor, her hands covering

her face. Griff drew Willa closer as he watched the older woman crying and rocking on the floor.

"Are you sure you're all right?" he asked Willa softly.

Willa rubbed her ankles. "I'm a little sore, but I'll recover." She glanced over at Clint's body. "This was all about revenge?"

"It sounds that way." He wrapped his arms around her and rubbed her back. "It's over now, sweetheart. You're safe." And it wouldn't have happened at all if he'd been doing his job, he thought grimly. He was asleep in the bed they had shared when these two had taken Willa.

He had failed her.

Willa burrowed closer. She was in Griff's arms, which was the only place she wanted to be. "I knew you would find me."

"I followed the car for a long time. They wouldn't have gotten away with you."

"I know that." She looked up at him, knowing that her love for him glowed in her eyes. "I knew you'd rescue me."

His face hardened. His arms tightened around her, then he set her away from him. "I need to call the police. It's going to take some time to get this straightened out."

Before she could answer, he picked up Clint's cell phone from the floor. He spoke quickly and tersely, then turned the phone off. "The police will be here in about ten minutes," he said.

Then Griff redialed, and she realized he was calling

his uncle. He told Ryan what had happened, and that Clint was dead. He listened for a long time, then he said, "I'll bring her home right away."

When he hung up the phone, his face was expressionless. "I'm going to take you back to the Double Crown Ranch. Ryan said he wants to make sure you're all right."

"You told him I was fine."

"I guess he wants to see for himself."

Griff turned away, and she heard the faint wail of police sirens. In a few moments, the tiny shack would be filled with people, and she wouldn't have a chance to talk to Griff for a long time. "Griff," she said, urgency in her voice, "promise me you'll come back to the ranch with me."

"I already promised Ryan that I would bring you home."

"I want you to promise that you'll stay there with me."

He scowled. "I'm not going to dump you there and keep going, if that's what you think. I'll have to talk to Ryan."

"That's not what I meant, and you know it. Promise me you won't leave until we have a chance to talk."

"Sure I'll talk to you. But there's nothing to talk about."

Her heart sank, but she reached out and touched his arm. "I think we have lots to talk about."

"We both have jobs waiting for us, Willa. We both

knew this wasn't going to last forever. You're safe now, and you can get back to your life.''

What if I don't want to get back to my life? Before she could ask him that question, the door burst open and police officers streamed in. One of them began asking questions, and Griff told them exactly what had happened. Another put a pair of handcuffs on Betsy.

Willa leaned against the wall of the shack and watched, suddenly weary. Her brain was still fuzzy from the drug she had been given, her hands and feet ached, and Griff was going to be difficult. She sank to the floor. She wasn't sure she could deal with anything right now. When one of the police officers appeared in front of her, she gave him her statement, then felt her eyes growing heavy.

She became aware of motion and a low, steady hum. Opening her eyes, she saw they were in Griff's truck, and they were driving down the highway. ''Where are we going?'' she asked, her voice still sleepy.

''We're going back to the Double Crown.''

She wrinkled her forehead. ''In the middle of the night? Why didn't we wait until tomorrow?''

''I figured you wanted all of this behind you as quickly as possible. And taking you back to your godfather's ranch was the best way of accomplishing that. Someone will go back to the cabin and fetch our things.''

"I'd hoped to have one more night in the cabin," she said softly.

There was a tense silence. "That wouldn't have been a good idea," he finally said.

"Why not?"

"You know why not, Willa." His voice was harsh. "What good would that do? We both know how this is going to end."

Her heart ached, but she refused to give in to the despair that threatened to engulf her. "I don't know how this is going to end, although I know how I'd like it to end."

"We were living in a dream world," he said roughly.

"It seemed very real to me." She couldn't bear to look at him. She was afraid she would see the hard, remote stranger he had been when they first met.

"We both know what's real, Willa."

She closed her eyes. She *knew* what they had was real. She just wasn't sure how to convince Griff. And she knew she couldn't do it now, in a car in the middle of the night. "Remember, you promised not to leave before we had a chance to talk."

"We're talking now."

"You're a man of your word, Griff. I'll talk to you at the ranch tomorrow."

She was still so tired that she could barely keep her eyes open. Leaning back against the seat of the truck, she slipped into sleep. But it was a restless one, broken by disturbing dreams.

By the time Griff touched her shoulder and told her

they were back at the ranch, fatigue weighted her arms and legs, and she wasn't sure she could climb out of the truck.

Ryan and his wife Lily, as well as Griff's brothers Reed and Brody and his sister Matilda, were waiting to greet them. Griff looked at her face and swept her out of the car. "Willa needs to sleep," he told them tersely. "Show me her room, and then we can talk."

She clung to Griff as he carried her through the house. She kept her eyes closed and concentrated on the sensation of being in his arms again. Too quickly, he set her down on a bed and stepped away.

"Go to sleep," he said, then his voice gentled. "There'll be plenty of time to talk when you wake up."

"You'll still be here, won't you?" she said, opening her eyes. She could see the hesitation in his face. "Promise me that you will, or I won't go to sleep."

Finally he said, "I'll still be here."

"I'll talk to you later then."

He turned and left, and Willa felt empty and alone. She yearned to feel his kiss again, ached for him to touch her. But he had walked out of the room without looking back.

She couldn't think about it right now. Her mind felt vague, and she suspected it was a side effect of the drug Clint and Betsy had used to knock her out. She needed to sleep. So she crawled beneath the sheets and closed her eyes.

Griff would be here when she woke up. He had promised that he would be.

And Griff always kept his promises.

* * *

Griff spent a long time talking to Ryan, glossing over what had happened between him and Willa at the cabin, but telling him all the details about Clint and Betsy. He accepted full responsibility for Willa's abduction, but Ryan brushed it off. "You got her back, and she wasn't hurt. That's all that matters."

It wasn't all that mattered, Griff thought. He had let Willa down, and Ryan, too.

"Betsy is in the custody of the El Paso police," he said stiffly. "She confessed to everything, including the fact that she was the one who'd shot at Mattie. She probably won't be charged with a crime in connection with Clint's death, because she saved my life and probably Willa's, not to mention her own. But I suspect she'll be charged with attempted murder for shooting at Matilda. The police told me she'd probably undergo extensive psychiatric testing."

Ryan shook his head. "Clint has hated all Fortunes since my father bought the Lockhart ranch from Clint's father. I had no idea he'd go this far, though."

"Has anyone told Mary Ellen and Jace that their brother is dead?" Griff asked.

Ryan nodded. "I called them both as soon as you told me what had happened. I called all of my children, too. After all, Clint was their uncle." The older man ran his fingers through his hair, and his face sagged. Suddenly he looked far older than his years. "I never meant for things to go this far. I didn't want Clint to die, even after all he's done. I suspected he was behind the attempt to abduct Willa, but I guess I was hoping he wouldn't go that far. Again.''

"It's not your fault," Griff said gently, seeing his uncle's distress. "Clint was mad. I saw it in his face, heard it in his voice. You couldn't have done anything to stop him."

Ryan leaned forward. "Thank God you were here, Griff. I never had a moment's regret or worry about putting Willa's safety in your hands. I always trust my instincts, and I knew you'd take care of her."

He'd taken care of Willa, all right. He felt his face harden. He'd forgotten his responsibilities and slept with her, and, as a result, she'd been abducted from right under his nose.

"I'm going for a walk," he said abruptly. "I have to clear my head."

"You've been up all night," Ryan said. "Don't you want to sleep?"

"I'll sleep later." It would do no good to try to sleep now. He would only lie awake and think about how he had failed Willa.

"Thanks again, Griff."

Ryan's words burned in his ears as he headed out of the house. "Hey, bro, where are you going?"

He heard Brody's voice behind him, but didn't slow down. "I'm going for a walk," he said without looking back. "I'll talk to you later."

"Oh, oh," he heard Brody say to Reed. "Griff is going walkabout again. What's happened now?"

Reed's answer faded in the distance behind him, and Griff just kept walking. If he walked far enough, and long enough, he might be able to erase the guilt that was eating away at him.

Willa woke up late in the day, feeling surprisingly refreshed. Daylight was fading as she swung her legs out of bed, and she realized she was ravenously hungry. Throwing on some clothes, she opened the bedroom door and saw Matilda sitting in a chair, reading a magazine.

Mattie jumped to her feet when she saw Willa. "We thought you were going to sleep around the clock," she said.

"I almost did," Willa admitted. "But my stomach woke me up."

Ryan's wife Lily appeared in the hall, and she smiled when she saw that Willa was awake. "I'll bet you're hungry," she said.

"I'm starving."

"Come to the kitchen and I'll fix you something to eat."

By the time they reached the kitchen, they had been joined by Matilda's new sisters-in-law, Mallory and Jillian. The four women insisted that she sit down, then brought her food and hot coffee.

After she had finished eating, Lily leaned forward. "You know we're all impatient to hear what happened," she said. A shadow passed over her face. "We know Clint is dead. Griff told us that much. But he didn't tell us anything else. Ryan's been on the phone all day, and your Griff's not very communicative, is he?"

"My brother is a clam," Matilda said bluntly. "But we know you'll spill the details."

Her Griff. The words gave Willa a warm glow, but she knew that Griff was by no means hers. He was going to be stubborn about what had happened between them. She knew him well enough to see that.

"Griff was wonderful," she began slowly. She looked down at her plate, but felt the knowing look that passed among Jillian, Mallory and Matilda. "Ryan sent him to College Station to check on the security at my apartment, and he arrived just in time to thwart Clint and Betsy when they tried to kidnap me."

Shocked exclamations filled the room, and Matilda covered Willa's hand with hers. "How awful," she said, her eyes dark with concern.

Willa gave them a shaky smile. "I guess it was, but it all happened too fast for me to be scared. Griff chased them off, then whisked me to the cabin near El Paso. We're still not sure how Clint and Betsy found us."

"I can tell you that," Lily said. "Ryan told me that Betsy confessed that she'd overheard a conversation between Griff and Ryan. When she told Clint about it, that was all he needed to hear. Clint knew all about the cabin near El Paso."

Willa stared at Lily, memories clicking into place. "Betsy worked here on the ranch," she said slowly. "I knew she looked familiar. She must have been wearing a wig when she came to the door."

Lily nodded grimly. "Apparently, Clint told her to

get a job with us so she could spy on us and keep him informed about what was going on.''

Willa looked over at Matilda. ''Is Clint the one who shot at you while you were on your honeymoon?''

''No, that was Betsy. But Clint put her up to it.''

Willa reached out tentatively and touched Matilda's hand. The younger woman immediately turned and clasped Willa's hand in hers. ''I'm so glad you're all right,'' Willa said quietly.

Matilda gave her a grin. ''So am I, mate.''

Suddenly Jillian gasped, then leaned back in her chair. Everyone turned to look at her.

''Are you all right?'' Mallory asked.

Jillian nodded, massaging her bulging abdomen and giving the other women a rueful smile. ''Sorry. I think this baby is saying that she wants to join the party.''

Mallory gave a radiant smile and laid a hand on the slight swell of her abdomen. ''I felt my baby kick for the first time just a week ago.''

Everyone turned to Mallory and began talking at once, and as Willa watched, a curl of envy snaked through her. It surprised her, because she'd never thought about having children before.

She'd never been in love before, either, she reminded herself. She had no idea how Griff felt about children. She had no idea how he felt about a lot of things. Including her.

Suddenly edgy, she pushed away from the table. The other women stopped talking and turned to look at her. It was now or never, she thought. If she didn't find Griff and talk to him, he would manage to get away from the ranch. And she would never see him again.

Gathering her courage, she said, "Does anyone know where Griff is?"

Mallory and Jillian gave her a slow grin. "So that's the way it is," Mallory said. "I recognize that look."

Matilda's eyes brightened. "Are you in love with Griff?"

Willa winced. "Are you always this blunt?"

"All the time," Matilda assured her. "You'd better get used to it if you're joining the family."

Willa felt tears fill her eyes. "I don't think that's what Griff has in mind. But I need to talk to him."

"My brother is a blockhead," Matilda said. "And I suspect he's gone walkabout. That's what he always does at home when he has a problem."

"Gone walkabout? What does that mean?"

Matilda laughed. "I guess you could translate it as a long walk. Sometimes he's gone for days. I'll send Brody and Reed to find him."

Willa followed Matilda out of the kitchen. As much as she liked Jillian and Mallory and Lily, she didn't want to face the understanding and pity in their eyes. She would wait outside, where the darkness could hide her tears.

Griff heard the sound of the truck engine in the distance, but he kept on walking. He didn't want to talk to anyone right now. He hoped that if he ignored whoever was driving out here, the person would leave him alone.

But the sound came closer, and soon he could hear his brothers' voices, calling to him. They had spotted him, and they weren't going to go away. Reluctantly he turned around and waited for them to reach him.

"What are you doing out here? Are you crazy?" Reed asked as the truck skidded to a halt.

"Go away," he answered wearily.

"After we went to all this trouble to find you?" Brody said. "Not a chance."

"I've been baby-sitting for the last week," Griff said coldly. "I'd like to be alone for a while."

Both his brothers looked him over, then they snickered at each other and nodded. "We heard about your baby-sitting job," Brody said. "Let's talk about that."

"Get lost," Griff snarled. "I'm not interested in talking."

"Get in the truck, Griff," Reed said, grinning. "It's two against one."

Thirteen

Griff took a deep breath, intending to tell his meddling brothers where to go, but he saw the concern beneath the laughter in their eyes. Sighing, he slid into the truck next to Brody, staring out the windshield as Reed put the truck into gear and pressed the accelerator. Griff braced himself as the truck bumped over the track through the pasture. They were heading in the direction of the house, but it would be a long drive. Griff had been walking for most of the day and into the evening. And he wasn't ready to go back to the house yet.

"Have you had your fun?" he finally asked his brothers. "Can I get out now? I told you, I want some time alone."

Brody looked over at him. "You never left us alone when *we* were in trouble. In fact, you're always the first one there when any of us need help."

"Who says I'm in trouble?"

Reed sighed. "Give it up, Griff. We saw your face when you drove in with Willa last night. If you're not in trouble, my last name isn't Fortune."

"My problems with Willa, or lack of them, are my business." His voice softened, because he knew his brothers were genuinely concerned for him. "There's nothing you can do, anyway."

Brody grinned. "Hell, Griff, if a brother can't meddle a little, who can? But we're not here to tell you what to do." He exchanged a look with Reed. "We simply came to find you because Willa needs you."

Griff shot upright in the truck, almost banging his head on the roof. "What's wrong with Willa? Is she sick? Did that bastard hurt her, after all?"

His brothers glanced at each other again, and Griff caught the look of understanding that passed between them. Then Reed said easily, "There's nothing wrong with Willa." He gave Griff a sly look. "At least, not physically that I could see. Her heart, now, that may be another story. Would you know anything about that?"

"There's nothing wrong with Willa's heart," Griff said coolly. "And if you're implying that I broke it, you're wrong."

"So you didn't break her heart." Brody's voice was too innocent. "Does that mean there's going to be another wedding in the family?"

Griff swore under his breath. "You're a couple of nosy—" He stopped himself. "Can't a man have some peace?"

"Maybe when you answer a question," Brody said mildly. "Have you called Mom and Dad and told them about the wedding?"

"There isn't going to be a wedding," Griff said, scowling out the window. "Is that plain enough?"

"You don't care about her, then." Reed's voice

was quiet, and he leaned back against the seat. "That wasn't the impression I got just a few minutes ago."

"You implied she was hurt or sick," Griff muttered. "What did you expect me to do?"

"Pretty much exactly what you did." Reed whistled as he drove expertly along the track, avoiding the potholes. "You'd be a fool to let her get away, you know."

Griff continued to look out the window. Finally he said, "It doesn't matter what I want. She's out of my league. I knew that from the beginning. I let myself forget it for a few days, but I won't forget again."

"I didn't get the impression Willa was the snooty sort," Brody said, his voice curious. "Is she really that much of a fool?"

Griff rounded on him. "Don't ever say anything like that again."

Brody laughed. "Just testing the waters, bro. Don't take my head off. I think Willa is just what you need. It's about time you found someone."

"Even if she'd have me, how can I ask her to share my life? I'm gone for months at a time. And when I leave, she'll never know if I'm coming back."

Brody and Reed exchanged a glance again. "We might have a solution to that little roadblock."

Griff stared out at the darkness, fear clenching his gut. He wasn't sure how Willa felt about him anymore. He'd let her down, failed her. He'd allowed her to be kidnapped.

"Are you paying attention, Griff?" Reed spoke sharply.

"I'm thinking."

"Well, you need to think about this...."

Griff forced himself to ignore the desperation inside him and listen to his brothers.

As they drove back, Reed and Brody outlined their plan.

The ranch house gleamed with light as they approached it, and when they reached the front porch, Reed stopped the truck. "This is where you get out," he said.

As soon as he'd closed the door of the truck, Reed hit the accelerator, and the truck disappeared around the corner of the house. Griff was left alone in the darkness.

But he wasn't alone, he realized a moment later. Willa was on the front porch. He shoved his hands into his pockets to prevent himself from reaching for her.

"How are you feeling?" he asked.

"Much better." She stayed in the shadows. "How about you?"

"I'm fine."

He couldn't see her, but he resisted the urge to move closer. Finally Willa said, "Why did you leave, Griff? Why did you leave me alone?"

"You weren't alone. As I recall, everyone on the ranch was fussing over you."

"That's not what I meant, and you know it. You were the only person I wanted to see, and you disappeared."

He closed his eyes, and the words seemed to burst from inside him. "I didn't think you would want to see me."

He felt Willa go still. "Why wouldn't I have wanted to see you?" she said, sounding puzzled.

"I let you down." He heard the self-contempt in his own voice and turned away to look out toward the darkened pastures. "I promised to protect you, but I allowed Betsy and Clint to kidnap you. Why would you want to see me?"

"You most certainly did not let me down." Willa's answer was prompt, and held a tartness that surprised him. "It was my own foolish fault that they were able to take me. You'd told me not to open the door to anyone, under any circumstances. And the first time someone came to the door, I opened it, anyway. How can that be your fault?"

"If I hadn't made love to you, hadn't spent the day and night in bed with you, I wouldn't have been asleep when they came to the door," he said roughly. "That is my fault."

"I think I may have had a little to do with the fact that you were sleeping. I don't think our lovemaking was one-sided."

"Hell, Willa, you're twisting my words. The bottom line is, I failed you. I wasn't there for you when you needed me."

"What happened was my own fault. In fact, I need to ask you to forgive me for not following your orders. By not listening to you, I put you in danger, too."

"I can take care of myself," he said gruffly. "You don't have to worry about me."

"But I do worry about you."

Willa watched as Griff took a step toward her. She held her breath, hoping that he would take her in his arms, but he stopped before he reached the edge of the porch.

"No one has worried about me for years." There was a hint of wonder in his voice.

"Nonsense," she said sharply. "I'm sure your mother worries about you every time you go off on one of your missions. To say nothing of your brothers and your sister." Her voice softened. "And now I'll worry about you."

"Willa," he began, then he spun around. "We're from different worlds. And when they intersected for a few days, I ended up letting you down. It would never work."

Willa wanted nothing more than to have Griff take her in his arms and tell her that he loved her. She yearned to hear him say that he never wanted to leave her again. But she could see he was determined. If she hesitated now, he would walk away and never look back.

So she swallowed hard and scrambled to find a less-threatening topic of conversation. She had to keep him here, keep him with her, until she could figure out a way to make him understand that she loved him and didn't want him to leave her.

And she knew she couldn't just tell him that she loved him. He'd claim it was some kind of stress-induced fantasy, some kind of rescuer–rescuee syndrome. And then he'd turn around and run, and he wouldn't stop until he was back home in Australia.

Moving casually over to the railing, she sat down on it and looked over at Griff. "So what are you going to do now that Betsy has been captured and Clint is dead? Are you off on another job?"

He gave her a suspicious glance, as if he wondered what she was up to. Then he shrugged.

"I told the El Paso police that we would be here at the ranch for a few more days, in case they had any more questions for either one of us. After that, I thought I'd see you back to your apartment in College Station and take care of those security measures that Ryan originally asked me to deal with. Once your apartment is as secure as it can get, I'll fly back to London. I have a lot to discuss with my boss."

Despair washed over Willa. Listening to Griff, she realized that he'd already put her in a compartment in his mind labeled To Be Forgotten. If he told himself that he didn't care about her often enough, he would begin to believe it. And he would never come back to Texas.

She took a deep breath and said, "I'm not going back to my apartment in College Station."

His expression was sympathetic. "I don't blame you. There are a lot of bad memories surrounding that apartment now. But I'm sure you'll be able to find another place. I'll help you look when I drive you back."

He'd dump her in the first place that looked halfway decent, then start running, she told herself. Looking him in the eye, she said, "You don't understand. Not only am I not going back to my apartment, I'm not going back to College Station or my job at the university there."

There was real shock on his face, but underneath it, she saw a glimmer of hope. "What are you talking about?" he asked.

She focused on that tiny ray of hope, and took a step forward. "Teaching at the university in College Station was never my dream," she said evenly. "It was always my father's dream for me. And because he was sick, I went along with him. But I won't be happy in that town for the rest of my life. I think I've known that all along, but now I'm willing to admit it. I'm going to resign my position there. I have other plans for my life."

Griff's eyes grew brighter. But he said, his voice harsh, "You worked damn hard to get that job. You can't give it up on a whim."

"It's not a whim, Griff. I've been restless and on edge ever since I agreed to take the job. I just wasn't able to figure out why. As soon as I made the decision to quit, it felt as if a load was lifted from my shoulders."

"What are you going to do?" He sounded as if he couldn't stop himself from asking.

"I'm not sure," she said. "Maybe I'll end up teaching somewhere else. I do love teaching—it's the only thing that got me through the last semester. But now, for the first time in my life, I'm going to do exactly what *I* want to do.''

"And what would that be?" he asked warily.

She didn't answer him immediately. It was time to go on the offensive.

"Griff, why did you throw yourself on top of me when you thought Betsy was going to shoot me?"

He gave her a startled look. "I thought she was going to kill you," he said. "Why would you even have to ask me such a thing? Of course I would try to protect you."

"If she had been trying to kill me, she would have shot you instead. You risked your life for me."

"Of course I did. I would do anything to protect you." He stopped abruptly, apparently realizing what he'd just admitted.

But it was too late. Willa had seen and heard the truth, and her heart eased in her chest.

"I would do the same thing," she said gently. "If the situation had been reversed, I would have given my life to save you."

"You can't feel that way about me, Willa," Griff said, and his tone was desperate. "You deserve someone far better than me."

"Oh, Griff," she said, stepping closer to him. "You're exactly what I need."

With a groan, Griff reached out and pulled her into his arms. His hands held her tightly, and she melted into him. Burying his face in her hair, he muttered, "I'm not good enough for you, Willa. I don't know if I can ever give you the stability and steadiness that you need.'' But his hold on her didn't loosen.

''I don't need stability and steadiness,'' she answered fiercely. ''All I need is you.''

Griff raised his head, and his eyes glittered in the moonlight. ''I'm not sure why, but I'm damn glad. But you'd better be sure, Blue. I won't let you go easily. You're everything I've ever wanted and didn't think I would ever find.''

He bent his head and kissed her, searing her with the intensity of his emotion. He kissed her like a dying man who had been brought back to life. His lips clung and held, telling her without words how much he wanted her.

And she answered him back in kind. She had been telling him no more than the truth—he was everything she wanted in her life. And she never wanted him to let her go.

He groaned deep in his throat and pressed her against the railing of the porch. She felt the tension in him, felt the desire quivering through him, and she wrapped herself around him. Her body yearned for his, yearned to be complete. And only Griff could complete her.

He slipped his hand underneath her sweater, and his fingers were hot and trembling against her skin. She pressed into him, urging him to take her. He groaned again as he caressed her back, feathering his touch down her spine, lingering at her waist until she burned and throbbed for him.

With shaking hands she began to unbutton his shirt,

needing to touch him, to feel him close to her. When she pressed her mouth against the hair on his chest, he bent his head to nuzzle her ear. But when she fumbled with the waistband of his jeans, he gently took her hands and held them away from him.

"Not here, Willa," he said softly. "Anyone could walk onto the porch at any time."

She pressed another kiss against his chest, then reluctantly rebuttoned his shirt. "I'm sorry. You're right."

He brought her hands up to his mouth. "Don't ever be sorry. You know I love to have you touch me. I just don't want you to be embarrassed."

Leaning against him, she wrapped her arms around his waist and looked away, knowing her face flamed with color. "You're right. I can't believe I…"

He chuckled in the darkness. "I learn something more about you every day, Willa. Will it always be that way?"

She looked up at him. "I don't know, Griff. Will it?"

He stared down at her for a moment, then he pulled her close again. "I love you, Willa. I love you more than I ever thought it was possible to love someone. When I saw you lying on the dirt floor in that shack, with Betsy and Clint standing over you, I thought for a moment that you were dead. And I wanted to die, too.

"Seeing you that way was the worst moment of my life. And when I saw that you were still breathing, it changed my life."

He eased away from her, and his face was hard and closed. "I don't deserve you, Willa." He held up his hand when she opened her mouth. "Don't say it. I don't care what you think—the truth is that I have stains on my soul that even you can't erase. But I love you. And because, by some miracle, it seems that you love me, too, I'm not going to let you go."

He paused, and a look of uncertainty came over him. "You do love me, don't you?"

"Of course I love you." She pulled his mouth down to hers and kissed him with all the passion in her soul. "I was afraid to tell you. I was afraid that you would start running and not stop until you were halfway around the world."

He gave her a crooked half smile. "Smart woman. I would have been gone so fast that there wouldn't even have been a vapor trail."

"I decided that I'd just hang around until you came to your senses."

"I'm glad you did." His smile faded. "I'm hard-headed, Willa. You can see how long it took for me to figure out that I loved you."

"Is this called truth in advertising?" she asked with a loving smile. "Am I going to have to catalog all my faults and failings, too?"

He scowled. "I just want to make sure you know what you're getting."

"Then I guess I should tell you that I'm very opinionated and bossy. I lose track of time when I'm involved in a project. And I'm very crabby until I get my coffee in the morning."

"That last one isn't news to me," he said, grinning.

She raised her eyebrows. "'I just want to make sure you know what you're getting,'" she mimicked.

He framed her face in his hands. "I love everything about you, Willa. Including your bossy, opinionated ways."

"And I love everything about you, including your hardheadedness." She grinned up at him as she wrapped her arms around his waist. "I imagine we'll have a few fights when your stubbornness comes up against my bossiness."

"I'll spend the rest of my life trying to make you happy, Willa. Will you marry me?"

She felt her eyes filling with tears. "Yes," she whispered. "Yes, I'll marry you, Griff."

He closed his eyes for a moment, then bent down and kissed her again. This time he kissed her lightly— a pledge and a promise. But when she put her arms around his neck and fitted herself against him, he groaned and set her away from him.

"How soon can we get married?" he asked hoarsely.

"I'd marry you tomorrow," she said. "But don't you want your parents to be here? And the rest of your brothers, and Mattie?"

He scowled. "I suppose they have to be."

She smiled. "And I know Ryan is going to want to throw a big wedding for me here at the ranch." She felt her eyes watering again. "He always told me that he was looking forward to my wedding. Since all of his children are married, he was counting on me to have an excuse for another big party.''

"I guess we can't disappoint your godfather,'' he said.

Willa leaned against him, holding him close. "I've waited for you all my life,'' she murmured. "I can wait a few more months, as long as you're with me.''

She felt him tense before he cleared his throat. "As a matter of fact, I won't be here for the whole time. I have to go back to London.''

She lifted her head. "That's right, you said you had to talk to your boss. Is it about your next assignment?''

Dread filled her heart, but she was determined not to let Griff see. His job was a part of who he was, and she wouldn't ask him to change it. But she knew she would worry about him.

"Not exactly.'' He looked down at her. "I'm going to resign. And I need to tell him in person. There are a lot of things to discuss if I'm leaving the department.''

She moved away and looked up at his face. "Griff, I don't want you to quit your job because of me. I know you must enjoy what you do, because you've been doing it for a long time. And I know from first-hand experience how good you are at it.''

"Willa, when I'm on an assignment, I'm gone for months at a time. I couldn't bear to be separated from you for that long. I wouldn't be able to contact you at all. You wouldn't know if I was dead or alive, and I wouldn't put you through that kind of worry.'' He drew her closer and gave her a reassuring kiss. "I was good at my job, but I have another focus for my life now. I want to come out into the light and stand in it with you."

"Are you sure?" she asked, then held her breath.

"Positive." His voice was firm. "I've just spoken with my brothers, and I'm going to go into the family business with them." He smiled at her. "There's even a small college not too far from our family ranch. I'm sure they would be interested in a very talented political science professor." His smile widened as he took her hands. "Do you think you could bear to live on a ranch in Australia?"

"I would love to live on a ranch in Australia, as long as you were there," she whispered. "That's all that matters, Griff. My home is wherever you are, because that's where my heart is."

"It's not going to be like Texas," he warned. "You'll be living on a ranch in the back of nowhere. We're an hour from that town with the college. There's no one around but family."

"You can't scare me away," she said, smiling up at him. "You're stuck with me now."

"I don't want you to regret this."

She moved closer, close enough to feel the tension that suddenly emanated from him. "How could I regret anything about us?" she said. "I love you." Her mouth curled into a grin. "And you know I like adventures."

"This is going to be one hell of an adventure for you."

"No, it's going to be an adventure for *us*. Marriage always is. But there's nothing I want more. I love you, Griff."

"And I love you, Willa."

He wrapped his arms around her, and she leaned against him. "It doesn't matter where we live," she whispered. "I'm already home."

Fourteen

"With this ring, I thee wed."

Griff's clear voice washed over Willa as she stood next to him in the inner courtyard of the house at the Double Crown Ranch. He slipped a heavy gold band onto her ring finger, then looked up at her.

The love in his eyes made her throat tighten. Then the minister spoke again, and without taking her gaze from his, Willa repeated the same words to Griff.

"With this ring, I thee wed."

Her hand trembled as she pushed an identical gold band onto Griff's finger. Griff turned his hand to hold hers tightly for a moment, then he brought her hand to his mouth and brushed his lips over their joined fingers.

The minister beamed at them. "I now pronounce you man and wife. You may kiss the bride."

Slowly Griff turned her to face him, then he bent his head and touched his mouth to hers. The caress was meant to be light and brief, but their lips clung and held as they melted together. Finally Griff pulled away, but he didn't let go of her hand.

"May I present Mr. and Mrs. Griffin Fortune." The minister smiled out at the people behind them.

She turned with Griff to face their relatives and

friends, and suddenly the courtyard erupted into wild clapping and cheering.

Griff grinned at her and leaned down to murmur in her ear, ''I guess that's what happens when you get a bunch of Australians and Texans together in one place.''

She slipped her hand through his arm and grinned back at him. ''I'd clap and cheer, too, if I thought I could get away with it.''

''You can do anything you want to do today,'' he replied, his eyes gleaming.

''Mmm. Hold that thought for several hours,'' she murmured.

As they walked down the narrow aisle between the chairs set up in the courtyard, he tightened the muscles of his arm, pulling her closer to him. ''Is that a promise?'' His voice was husky, sending shivers up her spine.

''You can count on it.''

By the time they reached the back of the courtyard and turned around, Griff's eyes held a promise of their own. But before she could lose herself in it, Matilda jiggled her arm.

''As matron of honor, it's my job to keep the bride from ogling the groom in the reception line,'' she said with a grin. ''Pay attention here, Willa. And you, too, Griff. There'll be a test later.''

Willa turned to Mattie with a smile, and gave her a quick, hard hug. ''Thank you for being my matron of honor,'' she said quietly. ''You don't know how much it means to me.''

Mattie's grin turned into a tender smile. ''I was

thrilled that you asked me,'' she said. ''And so was Junior.''

She laid her hand on her protruding abdomen, then gave both Willa and Griff a sly grin. ''And speaking of Junior, Dawson and I have some news of our own.''

''Did you find out the sex of the baby?'' Willa asked eagerly.

Mattie gave her a mysterious smile. ''Dawson and I will tell you later. This is your wedding day. We don't want to steal your spotlight.''

Willa was about to protest that she didn't mind, but then Ryan enveloped her in a huge bear hug. ''I can't believe my goddaughter is married,'' he said.

Willa clung to him for a moment, then stepped back so she could look at him. ''Thank you for letting us have the wedding at the Double Crown,'' she said softly.

''I wouldn't have let you have this wedding any-where else. This is where you belong. After all, you're my only goddaughter. You were a part of the family even before you married a Fortune.''

He turned to Griff. ''You're one lucky young man,'' he said.

Griff took his uncle's hand, and it looked to Willa as if both men held on longer than necessary. ''I know that, Uncle Ryan. I'll take good care of her.''

''I know you will, Griffin.'' Ryan squeezed his hand tightly, then let him go and slapped him on the back. ''And I'll expect to see both of you back at the Double Crown on a regular basis.''

''You will.'' Griff looked over at Willa and smiled.

"We've already talked about that. We'll come back to Texas several times a year."

"There will always be room at the ranch for you. And your children." He gave them a pointed look, and his wife Lily grabbed his hand to lead him away.

"You stop pestering Willa and Griff, Ryan. This is their wedding day. There's plenty of time to talk about children."

Ryan grinned at them over his shoulder as Lily pulled him away, and Griff leaned down to whisper in Willa's ear. "We'll have to discuss getting you pregnant, sweetheart. I think we have a lot of practicing to do."

"I'm a firm believer in the old 'practice makes perfect' adage," she whispered back.

Griff's eyes gleamed at her, but before he could say anything, another guest approached and gave him a hug. Willa waited, inhaling the fragrance of the blossoms that filled the courtyard, while the two chatted. Besides the cut-flower arrangements that had been brought in for the wedding, the area was overflowing with flowering plants that had begun blooming a few weeks earlier.

Spring in Texas filled the air with the fragrance of a thousand different plants coming back to life. The sky was a pure, sparkling blue and the air was warm as it blew gently across her face. April was the perfect time for a Texas wedding.

She and Griff hadn't wanted to wait that long to get married, but Ryan had been determined to throw them a big wedding, with all his friends and his family invited. He'd told them that since all his children were already married, Willa and Griff's wedding was the last one he'd have a chance to arrange for a long time. It would be a while before his grandchildren started to get married.

Besides, waiting a few months had given Griff's parents the chance to come to Texas for the wedding.

Fiona and Teddy stopped in front of Griff and embraced first their son, then her. "You're beautiful, Willa," Fiona said.

Willa saw the sheen of tears in her eyes.

She smiled at her son and his bride as she wiped her eyes. "Don't mind me. I always get weepy at weddings."

Griff hugged her again. "I'm glad you both could make it."

"We wouldn't have missed it for anything," Teddy said, clapping his son on the back and taking Willa's hand. "Your mother and I never thought we'd see this day. We were afraid you were going to spend your life roaming the world. I didn't think you were ever going to settle down."

"Is that what you call it?" Griff asked, his voice amused. "Settling down? I thought life on the ranch was more exciting than that."

Teddy's eyes twinkled. "We'll give you more excitement than you ever imagined," he said, slapping him on the back again. "Just you wait."

Fiona turned to Willa. "Have you heard anything more about that job at the college?" she asked.

Willa nodded. "I talked to them again last week. They sound very interested, but they can't offer me a job until they interview me in person. When Griff and

I come home after our honeymoon, I'm going to talk to them. If they offer me the position, I'll start teaching next semester."

"You'll get the job," Fiona said with an assured smile. "They'll see how lucky they would be to have you."

"Thank you." Willa felt herself blushing. She and Fiona had hit it off immediately. Fiona had taken Willa under her wing, helping her with the final details of the wedding, and Willa was still dazed with happiness.

All the Australian Fortunes had acted as if she were already one of them. Suddenly having four brothers and a sister was a bit overwhelming after being an only child all her life, but she loved every minute of it.

"Where are you going on your honeymoon?" Teddy asked.

"We're going to wander the world for a while." Griff glanced at Willa again and gave her a secret smile. "I've been a lot of places, but I haven't seen much. And Willa has an incurable travel bug. We'll be back at the ranch in a month or so."

"Take your time," Teddy said understandingly. "You haven't had a lot of time to yourselves the last few months, with the investigation and then the wedding to plan. And as much as I love it here at the Double Crown Ranch, it's not like there's a lot of privacy."

Fiona hugged Willa, then Griff. "We'll see you before you leave."

"You know we'll make sure we say goodbye to you," Willa answered.

Teddy and Fiona moved away, and another couple came up and gave them a hug. After a while, it felt like they'd been standing in the receiving line for hours, greeting friends and relatives. But Willa reveled in it. Even Griff didn't seem to mind.

But when the last of the guests drifted away, Griff turned to Willa. "I didn't think I'd ever have you to myself again."

"And you won't for another few hours," she said, reaching up to give him a quick kiss. "I want to find Mattie and Dawson. They had an ultrasound scheduled, and I think they've found out the baby's sex."

But before they could find Griff's sister, a baby started crying. They turned to see Brody and Jillian trying to ease their way through the crowds. Jillian was holding a red-faced, squalling Sarah. Their daughter was just two months old, and right now she looked very unhappy.

Willa hurried over to Jillian. "Is she all right?" she asked.

Brody grinned. "She's just hungry. And she doesn't like to wait."

"I'm going to find a quiet corner and nurse her," Jillian said. "I didn't want her to make a scene at your wedding."

"Don't be silly," Willa said immediately. "She's not making a scene. She's just hungry, aren't you, sweetheart." She cooed at Sarah, who stopped crying long enough to look at her with interest. "What a charmer you are."

"She takes after her mother completely," Brody agreed, wrapping an arm around Jillian and dropping a kiss on top of her head.

"Except for her stubbornness," Jillian added dryly. "That comes straight from her father."

The couple exchanged an intimate glance, then Brody eased Jillian through the crowds and into the relatively deserted house. Willa watched them go, then turned to Griff. "Sarah is such a darling," she said, knowing her voice sounded wistful.

"I can hardly believe I have a niece," he said, watching Brody and his wife disappear into the house.

"You're going to have two more nieces or nephews in a few months once Mattie and Mallory have their babies," Willa said, grinning at him. "By this time next year, there'll be a bunch of little Fortunes."

Griff smiled again. "We'll have to see what we can do to contribute."

Love tightened almost painfully in Willa's chest at the tender look in Griff's eyes. But before she could reply, she saw Reed and Mallory coming toward them.

Mallory was glowing, her gently rounded abdomen just visible beneath her maternity dress. "I can't believe you two aren't surrounded by people," she teased.

"We were just talking to Brody and Jillian. Sarah had decided she wanted to eat."

Mallory laughed. "Meaning, she was making a big enough scene to scare off the crowds."

"Something like that." Griff bent down to kiss her. "How are you doing, Mallory?"

"I'm great." She looked up as Reed joined her. "We're more than great. We had an ultrasound last week, and the baby is perfect."

"Did you find out the sex?" Willa asked.

Reed shook his head. "Nope. We don't want to know—we want to be surprised in four months. All we wanted to know was that the baby is healthy."

"We did pick out names, though," Mallory said.

"What did you decide?" Willa asked eagerly.

Reed grinned. "If it's a boy, he'll be Geoffrey Theodore after Mallory's father and mine. If it's a girl, she'll be Kyla Marie, because we just like the name."

Griff rolled his eyes. "Am I going to get as sappy as my brothers when we have a baby?" he asked Willa.

"You'll be far worse," she answered with a laugh. "The tough guys always are."

Griff laughed and gave her a kiss.

Then Willa listened as Griff and Reed talked about the business of the ranch in Australia. As they were talking, Ryan came up to them.

"I need to talk to all of you. I'm looking for Mattie and Dawson, and Brody and Jillian," he said. "Do you know where they are?"

"Jillian and Brody went inside so that Jillian could nurse Sarah," Griff answered. "I don't know about Mattie and Dawson."

"They're talking to Mom and Dad," Reed said. "Over there in the corner."

Everyone turned around to look. Fiona was wiping her eyes and smiling. Teddy looked stunned. "Whatever it is, it looks interesting,'' Griff said after a few moments.

"You can find out later," Ryan said. "Right now, I want to update all of you on Betsy Keene."

"Is she all right?" Willa asked.

Ryan gave her a strange look. "You act as if you're concerned about her."

"I am," Willa answered immediately. "She loved Clint, and she didn't realize what he had planned. And she did save my life and Griff's."

Ryan's eyes softened as he watched her. "I should have realized that's how you would feel. Come on." He herded them toward the house. "I don't want to interrupt your wedding, but I thought you would all want to know. Why don't you go into my study while I fetch Mattie and Dawson?"

After the noise and gaiety of the courtyard, the house felt still and silent. Reed, Mallory, Willa and Griff waited in the study, along with Jillian, Sarah and Brody, whom they had found preparing to return to the party. In a few minutes, Ryan ushered Mattie and Dawson into the room.

"I wanted you all to know what was going on with Betsy Keene, since you were all involved with her and Clint to one degree or another. She's still in prison and undergoing a psychiatric evaluation. I've talked to the psychiatrist, and he feels that there is a chance she might be released in another year or so. How do you all feel about that?"

"It doesn't bother me," said Mattie softly. "She did shoot at me, but it was Clint who made her do it. She loved him and that made her act irrationally."

"Love can't excuse everything," Dawson said, putting his arm around Mattie. "I'd want to be sure that she wouldn't try to hurt anyone again."

"I think that's what the psychiatrist has in mind," Ryan answered carefully. "Willa, how do you feel? She kidnapped you."

"She also saved my life and Griff's," Willa answered. "That should count for something."

Ryan smiled as he looked at her. "I figured you would say that. How about the rest of you?"

After they talked for a while, everyone agreed that if the psychiatrist felt that Betsy wasn't a threat any longer, she should be released from prison. Ryan looked at everyone, then stood.

"I'll tell the psychiatrist how you feel. It may not make a difference, but I'll let you know." He gave everyone a smile. "Now I'll let you all get back to the party. A wedding is no time to hide in the office."

They all started to follow him, but Mattie said, "Could you wait for a minute? Dawson and I have some news to share with you. We already told Mom and Dad."

"Is it something about the baby?" Griff asked.

"You could say that." Mattie grinned, then reached out for her husband's hand. "Dawson and I just found out that the baby is *babies*. We're having twins—a boy and a girl."

After a moment of stunned silence, everyone began talking at once. Finally Mattie held up her hand, laughing. "I'll tell you everything we know. Both of the babies are healthy, but I have to take it easy from now on. No riding or working with horses. We've already decided on names. The boy is going to be Colin, and the girl is Alyssa.''

"You're not naming the girl Matilda?'' Griff asked, giving her an innocent look.

Mattie picked up a throw pillow from the couch and tossed it at him. "I don't know how you put up with him, Willa,'' she said. "This baby will not be cursed with the name Matilda, or anything even closely resembling it. Alyssa is the most feminine name we could think of.''

The sounds of the reception echoed down the hall as Willa looked at Griff, standing with his arm around Mattie's shoulder. His two brothers stood on either side of him, their wives next to them.

"So much has happened in the last year,'' she said softly.

Griff moved to her side and hugged her. "The day Mom saw that news story about Bryan's kidnapping changed all of our lives. Teddy found his half brother Ryan, and we all found the loves of our lives.'' He brought Willa's hand to his mouth and gave it a lingering kiss. "Thank God she saw that story.''

"Amen to that,'' Brody said, taking Jillian's hand. "If we hadn't come to Texas, I wouldn't have found Jillian again. And I wouldn't have a daughter.''

"And I wouldn't have met Mallory,'' said Reed. He gave his wife an affectionate look. "And we wouldn't be expecting a baby in four months.''

"Heaven knows what would have happened to Mattie,'' said Brody with a teasing grin.

"She would still be giving me gray hair,'' said Griff. "Now she's giving Dawson gray hair.''

"It won't be long before Mattie will be on the receiving end in the gray hair department," Dawson said with a grin. "Wait until these twins start walking."

"Mattie is going to be a great mother," Willa said, smiling at Mattie. "Anyone can see that. A little thing like twins isn't going to rattle her."

"I've wanted children for a long time," Mattie said, beaming. "My prayers have been doubly answered. My only regret is that my family won't be closer."

"We'll be back in Texas all the time," Reed assured her. "With all the business ties we have with Ryan, one of us will be here about every month."

"And we'll go home regularly, too," Mattie said. "Especially now that the Australian Fortunes are part of the U.S. Fortune business. Dawson will have lots of reasons for going to Australia, and the twins and I will go with him." She gave her brothers a mischievous look as she laid her hand on her protruding abdomen. "From the way they've been kicking, I have a feeling that Alyssa and Colin are going to be bigger hellions than I was. They'll need their uncles to keep an eye on them."

Willa slid her arm around Griff's waist as she moved closer to him. "I can't believe that now I have not only four brothers and a sister, but nieces and nephews, too. I'm so glad you came to my apartment that day last December, Griff."

"I am, too," Griff murmured as he bent his head to kiss her. "Even though you were almost kidnapped that day, it turned out to be the best day of my life."

"And mine." She lost herself in Griff's kiss, and when she opened her eyes, she saw that the other couples in the study were exchanging kisses, as well.

"I'd say this trip to Texas has been the making of the Australian Fortunes," Griff said.

"You said it," agreed Brody.

Griff curled his arm around Willa. "Here's to Texas," he said, and he touched his head in a brief salute.

"And the happiness we all found," Reed said.

Griff put his arm around Willa's waist as all four couples headed out of the study and back to the reception. "The rest of our lives is waiting for us through those doors," he whispered.

"I can't wait to see what it holds," she answered.

They looked into each other's eyes for a moment, then turned to walk into their future together.

* * * * *

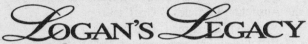

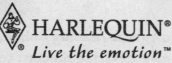

Coming in July 2004
from Silhouette Books

Sly McEwen's final assignment for top-secret government agency Onyxx had gone awry, leaving only questions behind. But Sly had a feeling Eva Creon had answers. Locked inside Eva's suppressed memory was the key to finding the killer on the loose. But her secrets may have the power to destroy the one thing that could mean more than the truth… their growing love for each other….

Available at your favorite retail outlet.

Forrester Square

LEGACIES . LIES . LOVE .

A story not to be missed…

In July, Forrester Square comes to a
gripping conclusion!

ESCAPE THE NIGHT

by top Harlequin Intrigue® author

JOANNA WAYNE

Returning to Seattle
after many years,
Alexandra Webber meets
Ben Jessup, who now lives
in her childhood home.
When recurring nightmares
and memories of a long-ago
night begin to haunt and
endanger Alex, Ben vows
to protect her.

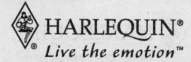

HARLEQUIN®
Live the emotion™

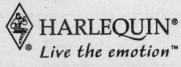